SUNCHASER

Emily Barlow

For my dad, who introduced me to fantasy and scifi at a young age and has always supported my reading and writing.

HUMBLE BEGINNINGS

Glorya of Farmer's Bend turned as she walked to watch the school, her home these past five years, recede into the distance. It didn't take long; once she was halfway through the mountain pass leading away from the small valley she could no longer see anything but the topmost row of dormitories cut into the far wall. Soon even those sank below the path's horizon and she was left with only the cold, sheer rock face on either side of the path for company.

She left much as she had arrived, with very little money, few clothes, and fewer possessions. The one new item she'd gained—the golden sun pinned to her rough-spun shirt—made the rest of her simple kit look even more plain in comparison, but brought out the highlights in her coppery hair. The sun had almost risen above the mountains to her left by the time she reached the end of the pass and was deposited unceremoniously into the scrubland beyond. Good, she thought. Plenty of time to reach Market. The corner of her mouth quirked in a near-smile as she used the downward slope to make better time toward her destination.

Despite clear weather and roads and the long daylight of summer, it was still nearly dark by the time she reached the small inn. Market supported only one, and it generally functioned only as a public house for the local residents; travelers were few, and most stayed only a single night. I'll fit in just fine in that respect. If she was lucky, no one would recognize her and she could avoid any social entanglements that might delay the rest of her trip. It had been a few years since she visited, and she'd grown and changed in that time—maybe enough to be hard to recognize.

Ducking through the single door, she cast a quick

look around the common room. Satisfied with the lack of acquaintances, she straightened to her full five-and-a-half-foot height and approached the innkeep, who doubled as a bartender most nights. "A room, please."

The innkeeper's countenance changed from passive observation to mild interest—the closest she would get to a smile. "Good to see you, Glorya. Passing through?" He took her payment and slid a room key over the bar.

"On my way to Fisherman's Watch to find work." She took the key. "Dinner still included?"

"Always. Might even have an extra crust of honeybread I can throw in for a local." He winked almost imperceptibly.

"I'd be most happy for it. It's been a long hike." Glorya put her pack down and had a seat at the bar. The innkeep disappeared into the kitchen, reappearing with a tray laden with a simple, hearty stew, golden beer, and a thick slice of dense, dark bread dripping with honey. Glorya bent her head to the meal, realizing she was hungrier than she'd thought, and before long was sleepily polishing off the last bits of honeybread. She thanked the innkeeper, took her key, and trudged up the stairs to her room, where she fell asleep fully clothed, pack in hand.

The next morning Glorya set out down the fishermen's road to the coast. It was another hard day's travel to Fisherman's Watch, the port town that might hold an opportunity to make a name for herself—or at least a living, she corrected mentally. She was almost out of money, and before long the need to eat would override any desire for notoriety. Her best hope was to check with the portmaster to see who, if anyone, might be in need of her services.

The weather was balmy and warmed perceptibly as she

neared the coastal town, moist saltiness gathering gently on the exposed skin of her face and arms. By late afternoon she was staring at the collection of haphazard streets and buildings that had grown up at the apex of the large bay before her. The strong breeze was funneled toward her through the twisting streets, smelling of brine, fish, and humanity. Simply-dressed people strode purposefully into and out of town carrying baskets or leading beasts of burden, and more than once she was forced to step aside to let laden carts pass both directions. No one seemed to take much notice of her. I wouldn't, either, she thought as she checked her purse before heading into the sea of trade and commerce that was Fisherman's Watch.

Glorya had only had reason to visit town once, when she was a child; her father had traveled an extra day to meet with a trader who'd promised a selection of seeds from downcountry. When they'd arrived he'd demanded twice the quoted price, and her father had walked away empty-handed and angry. She remembered sleeping on his back as he'd trudged back to Market to avoid paying the inn fees in Fisherman's Watch.

She snapped out of her reverie just in time to notice the sign for the inn where her father had met the merchant. Better find the port before finding room and board. She wasn't sure how far her purse would go in the port town. Faced with unfamiliar surroundings and a crossroads, Glorya stopped for a moment to orient herself. She'd arrived from the east; to the south the buildings grew cleaner and taller just before rounding a corner; to the north, a few buildings, then shanties; and to the west she could feel the source of the breeze's humidity. Docks are that way. She lost no time striding toward the lowering sun in hopes the portmaster would still be at work.

Two streets later she seemed to have turned completely around. The sun was now behind her, and the wind had traded the smell of fish for unwashed humanity. She resolved to ask the next person she saw how to get to the portmaster's building.

Glorya rounded a corner—and almost ran into a woman standing outside one of the nearby shops. Apologizing nervously, she took stock of the woman, who was leaning toward her a little drunkenly and wearing a tight-fitted bodice that barely contained a very ample bosom. "Very sorry, ma'am, but can you tell me where the portmaster's office is? I seem to be lost."

"The portmaster, eh? Looking for 'im?" the woman cackled, sharing a glance with another similarly-clad woman across the street. "Afraid you won't find the portmaster in this town."

"No," called the woman across the street, "but if you ask nicely we might just give you a place to stay for the night—for a small price…" The woman winked suggestively.

Glorya swallowed, remembering herself. "No thank you, I simply wish to find the portmaster."

The first woman peered at her, amused. "You ain't been here afore, 'ave you? Wouldn't know that it's a portmistress ye're seeking, lass. You look like a kind soul, so I'll give ye this for free: if you turn 'round and go two streets down, then take a left, ye'll find yerself at the wharf. Ask whomever ye sees for the portmistress and they'll show you right." The woman winked at her. "And come back if ye're in need of some company tonight; it's not often we see hair like that on a young body like yerself." As Glorya looked on, both women sashayed over to the next person down the street, a rough-looking young man.

Swallowing again, she turned on her heel and followed the woman's directions, hoping desperately that they were reliable. Two streets and half the distance to sundown later she found herself facing the office of the portmistress of Fisherman's Watch. She knocked politely.

"Enter." The no-nonsense voice shot through the worn wood of the door as if it wasn't there. Glorya turned the weathered knob with a barely-shaking hand and obeyed before she could even consider her actions.

The room before her was small and completely bare of adornment, much like the woman behind the simple table at the far end. Unsure of what she'd been expecting, Glorya was still surprised to find an elder woman before her, tall and stout of build, with her long hair swept back in salt-crusted yellow braids. Her tanned and weathered skin bespoke a lifetime at sea before her present work, which bent her over a large tome. She didn't even look up before addressing Glorya. "State your craft and cargo."

Inhaling deeply to find her voice, Glorya answered, "Portmistress, I am looking for work and was told you might direct me to a ship in need of my services." It all came out in a rush despite her best efforts at composure.

"Fishing boats will be coming in with the tide in an hour or so. Look there." The woman continued working at the figures in her book.

"I thank you, portmistress, but I am looking for trade ships."

"None of those in port today, and most have deckhands aplenty." More scribbling.

"While I am able of body, I am not seeking a deck-hand's work." Glorya took two steps closer to the desk. "I come from Weatherwatch."

The portmistress looked up sharply from her book.

"Oh." She snapped the dusty volume closed in a cloud of ink-sand. Scratching her head between two of her braids, she considered Glorya for a moment. "You look able; they might have more use for you than some of the others who've come through. What experience do you have?"

"None, portmistress. I'm newly graduated, first in my class." Glorya's chin rose slightly.

"And your skill?"

"Sunchasing, portmistress."

The portmistress's head cocked to the side in silent thought. After an uncomfortably long moment meeting Glorya's gaze, she said slowly, "I have nothing today…" she trailed off as Glorya's posture slumped perceptibly, "…but check back tomorrow. Two ships are due from the south, and they're in need of services such as you can offer." Glorya let out a breath she hadn't realized she was holding. "Now, off with you; I must finish these figures before taking my meal." Opening the tome back to the page she'd left, the portmistress turned her full attention back to the numbers before her, an obvious dismissal.

Glorya thanked the woman, then backed out the door with as much aplomb as she could muster while shaking with relief and exhaustion. She suddenly realized she was starving; she'd last eaten while on the road into town, and her supply of food was now exhausted. She would have to find an inn for the night. Looking around, she saw a sign down the row that showed a picture of a bed and utensils. It looked humble, but she could hardly afford to be picky. Trudging down the street to the door of the inn, she entered and asked the barkeep the price of lodgings for one night. He answered, and she reached for her purse—only to realize it no longer hung at her hip. The face of the leering woman flashed into her mind, and she pushed down a wave of anger and shame at her own naivete. Thanking the barkeep, she pushed aside her hunger and made her way determinedly back out of town to find a place to camp for the night.

The terns woke her before dawn. Glorya rubbed the salt from her eyelashes; she'd found a place among the dunes north of Fisherman's Watch that was hidden from both the road and the beach and had made a bed out of seagrass and her mostly-empty pack. Rousing herself fully, she took care of nature's call, then ignored her rumbling stomach and headed back into town.

When she arrived back at the portmistress's office not long after dawn she found the door already open and the woman about the day's business. Nodding to Glorya, the portmistress remarked, "You're an early riser. Good; speaks well for your work ethic. Come help me with these books, will you? First merchant isn't due until midmorning, so might as well make yourself useful." She appeared to be boxing up large tomes like the one sitting on the desk from yesterday.

Glorya went to work helping box up volumes and manifests without complaint. The portmistress talked as she worked, which helped the time pass quickly, and before they both knew it the sun was high in the sky. Stopping for lunch, the portmistress shared her simple fare of cheese and bread, which Glorya did her best not to bolt down out of politeness. It wasn't quite enough to fill her growling belly, but it was far better than the nothing she'd planned on. *I could stand to lose a few pounds, anyway.*

The portmistress looked out the door at the angle of the sun, squinting out at the horizon. "Southern Sun should've been here by now." She strode back inside and flipped through the pages of her book, nodding to herself.

"Must've run afoul of something. No matter; the Serpent is due back today, as well."

As if on cue, a tall, broad, black-bearded man knocked on the open door, doffing his workman's cap. "Begging your pardon, portmistress—I'm Jim, quartermaster of the Serpent, here with our cargo manifest." Ducking through the door he handed a sheaf of papers to the portmistress, who nodded.

"Someone here to see you," she replied, jerking her head toward Glorya. "She's looking for work. Think she'd do well on your southern route."

The man seemed to notice Glorya for the first time, blinking owlishly as he took stock of her appearance. "What be your skill?" he asked, noticing her gold pin.

"Sunchasing," she replied, standing a bit straighter.

"Southern route's hard work for the likes o' you," the quartermaster replied. "Plenty of storms come up quick-like, strong ones, too."

"I graduated first in my class," Glorya answered. "Haven't met a storm yet I couldn't tame."

"It's two months' journey with three stops, then a week back here to Fisherman's Watch. You'd bunk with the crew; no such thing as privacy aboard the Serpent. And we might need an extra hand with duties on occasion." He paused. "You look able enough."

"I'm no stranger to hard work."

"Can't pay what the bigger merchant vessels can."

"Can't build a reputation on nothing."

Apparently satisfied, the quartermaster nodded, offering his hand. Glorya met his eye and shook his hand with all the firmness she could muster, which was considerable given her farm upbringing and skill with a blade. Jim the quartermaster grinned. "We're glad to have you. Gather

13

your things and meet me at the dock in an hour–we'll be unloaded by then and you can meet the cap'n." He nodded to the portmistress and took his leave.

"Thank you," Glorya began, but the woman forestalled her with an upraised hand.

"Thank me not until you know what you've signed up for. The southern routes are plagued with storms this time of year. The Serpent will be very lucky to have you, but be careful you don't bite off more than you can chew."

Thirty minutes later Glorya was waiting on the dock by as large a vessel as she'd ever seen. It had two masts with striped green and white sails and a stylized serpent for the figurehead, its curved tongue licking the bowsprit. Deck hands were using cranes attached to the wharf to haul boxed cargo from the wharf into the hold amidships, and she could hear men in the cargo hold calling up to the ones working the cranes. Other crew members were checking rigging, tying knots, splicing ropes, and mending the sheets. Watching the buzz of activity was enough to keep her busy as she waited for the quartermaster.

"Never been aboard one, eh?" The voice behind her made her jump. The Serpent's quartermaster stood behind her, laughing jovially at her startlement. "Can always tell a first-timer. Don't worry, the magic wears off within a week." He was carrying more papers and a few small boxes. "Cap'n should be along shortly. Wait here." Jim strode up the gangplank and toward the captain's cabin under the quarterdeck, disappearing through a set of double doors.

Glorya waited, her pack slung over one shoulder, and did her best to look like she belonged.

Ten minutes later a middle-aged man with brown hair in faded green silk came striding up the wharf toward the ship. A whistle blew somewhere on the deck, and there was a sudden flurry of activity as men and women appeared from various places and lined up by the gangplank. Unsure of what to do but certain something important was occurring, Glorya stood a bit straighter right next to the wharf side of the gangplank.

As he got closer, Glorya could tell that the man wasn't walking entirely straight. She wasn't sure if it was just his gait or he was hung over—or perhaps still drunk—but he failed to make eye contact until he nearly tripped over Glorya's shoe in his rush to board the ship, at which point he staggered backward, a cloudy expression covering his face. He raised a finger to admonish and stopped abruptly when he realized the face before him was new.

"Glorya Sunchaser, at your service." She capitalized on the moment in hopes that it would help her avoid an apparent scolding.

The man's mouth opened, closed, opened again, and he lowered his finger. "Captain Danee of the Serpent at yours," he finally replied. "You're the one Jim hired?"

"The same."

"Well, then, get aboard!" He gestured for her to follow him as he started unsteadily up the gangway. Glorya followed, wondering if she should be ready to catch him at any point.

As soon as he was aboard, the whistle sounded again and the captain made some sort of gesture, at which point everyone went about their business. He turned back to Glorya as two deck hands finished loading the last of the cargo in the hold and pulled up the gangplank. "Jim can help you find your bunk. We cast off with the tide, which should be in about—" he started to gaze up at the angle of the sun, then thought better of it—"well, soon." Turning on his heel, he took a rather too-large step, then strode off toward his cabin, closing the double doors behind him.

Glorya stood amid a flurry of activity. The deck was crawling with crew—men and women climbing the rigging, in the crow's nest, on the deck, tying things down, yelling to one another. One in particular seemed to be directing this whirlwind from atop the quarterdeck. He was a man of advanced age, white beard streaming in the light breeze, strong baritone voice booming directions across the deck, none of which made sense to Glorya. His wiry arms moved and pointed and the sea of crew members shifted to follow. Glorya thought she might get completely lost in the shuffle and did her best to stay out of the way, dodging ropes and crew and making her way toward the shelter of the ship's forecastle.

Finally the whistle blew again and the heavy ropes holding them to the docks were cast off, leaving the boat to drift until a command was given and the sails unfurled, catching the stiff wind off the bay. From her vantage point it was an impressive sight, especially for a farm girl.

Just then she saw Jim appear from across the deck. He cast about for a bit, then caught her eye and motioned for her to join him by the quarterdeck. The ship had started to shift as they tacked out of port, and Glorya found it difficult to make a straight line, but she eventually navigated the bustling deck and joined the quartermaster.

"What do you think so far?" he asked once she was in earshot.

"I think I have a lot to learn," Glorya replied. "But at least the weather will be nice."

Jim laughed and clapped her on the back. "There's hope for you yet! Let's get you below and stow your things." He guided her to a door she hadn't noticed next to the captain's cabin that led belowdecks.

A narrow staircase took them down into the first level, which was open forward to where the mainmast delved below the deck. Rows of bunks swung gently between stanchions, with small chests underneath for personal effects. Many looked to be in use, but a few near the staircase were empty, their chests open. Nobody wants to sleep near the stairs; I wonder why? The quartermaster gestured toward the bunks. "This is where the crew sleeps. Feel free to find an empty one and claim it for yourself. Only toilets are abovedeck, on the bowsprit, so make sure you go before bedtime." He waited for her to deposit her pack in one of the chests on the second row from the staircase—must be a reason no one wants to sleep there—then led her on a tour of the ship that would be her home for the next two months.

Glorya was fascinated. The actual cargo hold was on the second level down and carried the ship's goods between the mainmast and the foremast, or amidships, as she learned from the quartermaster. Under the forecastle—fo'c'sle, she reminded herself—was supply storage for repairs and other things necessary to keep the ship running throughout its journey. She was introduced to the cook and a few other crew members, all of whom were polite, if wary of the newcomer.

Before long they had arrived back on deck via the forecastle stairs. "Begging your pardon, but I need to be about my own duties," Jim said. "I'll leave you with the bosun. He'll make sure you know where to be and when you're needed—and probably rope you into some choring, too." They crossed the deck again, which was gaining a rhythm to its pitch and yaw. Glorya noticed that however much the deck moved, Jim's head didn't, and she wondered at his ability to navigate the swells so efficiently.

Up on the quarterdeck, the elderly man was still directing the crew's activities, though with much less animation
than before. He turned as they approached and nodded to
Jim. "Quartermaster."

"Bosun. I've got you a new crew member—this is
Glorya Sunchaser." Glorya ducked her head respectfully.
"She's a bit green, but should keep us safe this journey."

Faded blue eyes regarded her critically. "Sunchaser,
eh? I've worked with your like a few times before. Going to need you abovedecks most of the trip. You afraid
of heights? Any problems climbing?" Glorya shook her
head. "We'll have you climbing the rigging soon, then.
You look able, so might need your help elsewhere as well.
How's the weather looking for the next while?"

Glorya closed her eyes for a moment, then opened
them and turned in a circle, gazing across the horizon.
"Should hold for at least the next few days unless something changes."

The bosun nodded. "I'm trusting you to keep a weather
eye at all times. Since things look quiet for now…" He
squinted around the deck, his gaze settling on a well-
built, clean-shaven man with tousled brown hair just
a few years older than Glorya. He pointed. "Go speak
with young Henrick, there. He'll get you settled. Now if
you'll excuse me…" The bosun nodded respectfully and
set about organizing another group of crew. Jim took his
leave as well, leaving Glorya staring down from the quarterdeck at her next assignment.

Henrick turned out to be a fount of information on the
ship, its crew, and the jobs necessary to keep it going. He
had been raised on a farm, as well, so Glorya felt more at
ease than she had with the rest of the crew she'd met thus

far. They walked around the deck as Henrick explained the ongoing tasks, the names of the portions of the ship, and his particular role abovedecks. Before long he was teaching Glorya how to climb the rigging in hopes she would be able to keep watch from a higher vantage before their journey was done.

Dinnertime snuck up on Glorya. The meal was served in the mess belowdecks for anyone not on duty, which included her. It consisted of plain fare, but was filling and warm, and she found herself getting sleepy after the first full stomach she'd had in two days. The bosun, or simply Bosun as everyone referred to him—she hadn't heard a proper name for him yet—came to let her know that she was welcome to sleep the night shift, but would be awoken if any sign of adverse weather appeared. She'd be expected on the quarterdeck at dawn.

The next two weeks passed uneventfully. Glorya would wake at dawn with the changing of the shifts, head up to the quarterdeck, check on the weather, and find Henrick, who would give her a job for the day. As soon as he learned she had experience on a farm he'd set her to mending ropes, rigging, and nets, and that had kept her busy for a few days. Even the taciturn Bosun, who rarely showed any sign of emotion, had nodded appreciatively at her work.

The third week saw them approaching their first port destination. It was a small town to the south, much like Fisherman's Watch, and they wouldn't be staying long; just long enough to offload cargo and take on more supplies and goods for trade in the southern cities. As soon as the Serpent had cuddled up to the wharf, Captain Danee had materialized from his cabin, left the ship, and returned again before the tide went out, clearly intoxicated. The crew largely seemed to ignore him beyond the traditional deference due a captain, looking instead to the Bosun for their direction and leadership.

Their second port of call was two days out when the first storm appeared on the horizon. Glorya was in the midst of learning to tie a knot when the call came from the crow's nest. "Dark clouds on the horizon, sir!"

Dropping her rope, Glorya climbed the rigging halfway up the mainmast with passable aplomb to get a better view. Sure enough, the sky showed a bruised blue-black off the starboard bow far in the distance. Her training at Weatherwatch returned unbidden. "We must only interfere when life or livelihood are in peril, and even then, to the lowest degree necessary." Twisting her foot into the rigging in case of unpredictable swells, Glorya closed her eyes and extended her senses to find the storm.

There it was—miles away, feeding off the warm southern seas. It wasn't a large system—yet—but it was likely to bring wind and heavy rain.

Finding her way back down the rigging and onto the quarterdeck, Glorya found the Bosun. "How much pitch can the Serpent take loaded as she is?"

Bosun considered for a moment before answering. "About so," he indicated with an upraised arm at an angle. "Anything more and we'll take on too much water. Or lose a mast."

Glorya nodded. "I'll see what I can do." Her mind was already racing over the exercises necessary to reduce the storm to a navigable degree while preserving the weather system as a whole. No reason to deny a farmstead their rainfall if I can help it. Climbing partway up the rigging, she settled herself against the foremast this time, twining both feet into the ropes for stability, facing into the wind.

By now the storm was close enough to smell. An electric feel slid over the ocean ahead of them as thunder rumbled in the distance. Glorya closed her eyes and let her awareness drift into the storm. Her earlier estimation was right: it was feeding off of the warm southern waters. Its rapid growth was generating more wind than the ship could handle, and the lightning it spat at the ocean would endanger the crew.

That was all she needed to know. Drawing on her willpower, she started to take the storm apart bit by bit. The growing clouds, the charged particles in the air, the rapid movement of the wind across the ocean—every part of the storm was hers to manipulate. Mentally she put up walls between clouds, disallowing their combination and the formation of the thunderhead growing at the front of the system. She blocked the charged particles from connecting, heading off the lightning before it could form. With the reduction of the system the wind slowed to a manageable level, and by the time the Serpent hit the once-tumultuous waters beneath the clouds, a gentle rain was falling.

As a gentle wind filled the sails, the deck went strangely quiet. Glorya descended the rigging and trudged back up to the quarterdeck, tired enough not to notice that the crew made way for her as she crossed the main deck. Bosun gave her a full salute as she crossed the quarterdeck. "You've made your pay today, and no mistake," he said as Glorya leaned against the railing. "Go see the cook. You'll be in need of some sustenance." With that, he shooed her off the quarterdeck. "What're you all lookin' at? There're chores to be done!" As abruptly as it ended, the bustle of the main deck began again as Glorya disappeared below.

They made their next port with no further incidents.

Glorya noticed the crew gave her a bit of a wider berth whenever possible, and most treated her with more deference than they had before she'd calmed the storm. Henrick, however, seemed not to have noticed. He continued to work with her and instruct her as if nothing had happened, which comforted Glorya as the days passed and some of the crew became more distant.

This time, they stayed in port for a few days. Captain Danee debarked immediately, as he had each time before, but portions of the crew also made their way into the town in shifts once the cargo was unloaded. Henrick asked Glorya if she'd like to see the town with him, since she'd never visited anywhere this far south and could use a guide. She agreed a little more eagerly than she'd intended to, telling herself she was simply excited to see what the town had to hold. Placing her hand in his arm, they strode down the gangplank and off into the unfamiliar streets.

They spent the remainder of the day exploring the market district. Glorya's senses were overburdened by the abundance of smells, sights, and sounds, each more exotic than the last. This, she thought, this is what Father was after when he came to Fisherman's Watch. There were cloths of all colors, jewelers with brightly-colored gems, tinkers fixing everything imaginable, carts brimming with foods she couldn't name...Glorya reveled in the unfamiliarity of it all. Henrick grinned as he watched her take it all in, memories of his first voyage south almost visible in his eyes as he saw the market with new eyes once again.

Sometime after sunset they made their way back to the ship, laughing and talking more easily than Glorya had in weeks. They sat abovedecks for another hour or two, sharing stories of childhood, schooling, and training for sailing. Henrick hoped one day to become a bosun himself, while Glorya wished to see herself distinguished for her craft.

Finally the warmth of the evening caught up with them both, and Glorya found herself nodding on Henrick's shoulder. He poked her a few times, then walked her down to her bunk. She barely remembered his soft "Good night" as she fell into sleep.

Two more days in port saw the hold fuller than Glorya had seen it. Most of their cargo was crates of indeterminate origin and contents, but occasionally she caught a glimpse of what they were carrying: silks, spices, dried fruit of a type she'd never seen...she didn't dare go into the hold to peek, but the smells from the crates told a story. Before she knew it the hold was full to brimming and they prepared to set sail. This time she was allowed to help cast off as they headed ever southward. Henrick continued to teach her seamanship, though she became acutely aware of his presence anytime he was nearby. They had made a habit of finishing their duties early enough to take dinner together belowdecks most days, a ritual she looked forward to with wary eagerness.

Their final port of call was four days' journey when the call came from the crow's nest. "Wind's pickin' up, Bosun! Clouds off to starboard!" Glorya swarmed up the rigging with confidence, winding a foot into the ropes and throwing herself into the oncoming storm.

The fierceness of the weather system lashed out at her senses almost immediately. What looked like a regular storm at a distance was, in fact, a hurricane. She'd read about them at Weatherwatch, but never encountered one, sheltered as the school had been by the fjords. It spun like a top, leaving waste and death in its wake across both ocean and land, and resisted any tentative probe she made to plumb its depths with an almost sentient tenacity.

Pulling herself out of the storm for a moment, Glorya

buried a second foot into the rigging. She shouted to be heard over the crew's bustle and oncoming wind. "Hurricane off starboard! I'll do what I can, but make ready!" Taking a spare rope she kept hanging from her belt, Glorya lashed herself to the foremast and dove back into the storm.

She was better prepared for the battery of natural force this time, but it still rocked her as she reached the edge of the system. It seemed to have a mind of its own, spinning clockwise as fast as its wind would carry it. Every time Glorya found a chink in the system, it slid away from her in an exhausting game of cat-and-mouse. She could feel her strength draining; the warm water below fed the storm and fanned the already-lethal gale, but she had no similar well from which to draw.

Suddenly she had an idea. It wasn't in any of her textbooks, and she was entirely unsure if it would even work, but it was her only hope of gaining any semblance of control over the cyclone. Instead of trying to separate the parts of the storm, she cut it off from the warm updrafts feeding it. Once it was no longer drawing strength from the ocean she was able to slow the churning of the clouds and winds until the hurricane began to break apart into smaller systems, each still dangerous in its own right. Fortunately only one lingered in their path, and with the last of her strength she fragmented it enough for the Serpent to pass through with moderate safety. Their passage thus assured, she slumped against the foremast, unconscious.

She awoke in her bunk, still damp with sea spray and rainfall. Opening her eyes rewarded her with stabs of sunlight filtering down through the open door and into her tender skull. That's why nobody takes these bunks.

Closing them again, she sat up carefully to take stock of herself.

Her ankles were a mass of bruises. One was twisted and the other felt tender, but sound. A ring of bruises adorned her waist where she'd lashed herself to the mast. At least I know the ropes held. She vowed to thank Henrick for his insistence in her learning knotwork. Her head felt as if it weighed a ton and her tongue was swollen in her mouth.

Glorya gingerly got to her feet, then used the stanchions as supports on her way to the galley to find food. She was met halfway by Jim Quartermaster carrying a mug and a plate. "Sit down, Sunchaser," he said as he ushered her back to her bunk. "You've had a hard day. Here, eat something." As she sat down he handed her the plate and the mug, which contained salt pork, porridge, and a dark beer, respectively.

"What time is it?" she asked around a mouthful of pork.

"About an hour after sunrise, the day after the storm," the quartermaster replied. She stopped chewing for a moment and stared at him.

"I've been unconscious for a day?"

"Yes, and it was touch and go for a bit there. Bosun himself looked after you for a bit after Henrick pulled you down out of the rigging." He continued to talk through the blush she couldn't suppress. "Bosun says he's never seen the like. He's the only one of us has seen more than one of your kind, and he thought we were done for soon as he heard 'hurricane.' So far's he knows, what you just did has never been done before." The quartermaster stood and saluted, causing the blush to deepen against her slowly tanning skin. "I'm sure the crew would like to see you up and about if you're up to it."

Finishing her porridge, Glorya nodded and took the quartermaster's proffered arm.

Her first impression of the deck was that it was bright—too bright to see. The sun was out in all its blazing glory, and while the knives in her head had subsided, there was still a dull throb. Her second impression was that it was noisier than usual. Once she was able to process the glut of sensory input she realized that most of the crew was on deck...and they were cheering. Jim the quartermaster's face split in a grin as he led her up to the quarterdeck, where Bosun was waiting with another salute.

"Sunchaser."

"Bosun." She nodded carefully, testing her head, and found that she was able to move it without as much pain.

"Good to see you up and about. Thought we might've lost you, though you saved both us and the ship."

"Never met a storm that was my match," Glorya replied. "Hope I never will."

Four days later they put in at the last and largest port on their route. As expected, Captain Danee appeared for the first time in days as soon as they hove to, but instead of heading directly for the gangplank, he turned toward Glorya quite a bit more steadily than he'd managed prior. "Sunchaser, I hear I have you to thank for the lives of my crew and the survival of my ship. I reviewed your wages for this journey and found them short of your deserve, so in light of recent events I've decided to double them. If you wish to stay on I will pay that now plus your original wages when we return to Fisherman's Watch, but if you should desire to find other employment here I will gladly vouch for your ability with the portmaster or any other captain on top of your pay. The choice is yours."

Glorya looked around at the crew's faces. Most were hopeful; some held outright adulation. Henrick's open countenance was tender and sad, as if he knew her answer already. "I came to find my fortune, Captain," she replied, tearing her gaze away from Henrick's. "It seems I have a good start. If you're willing to let me stay here, where work is more plentiful for me, and give me good reference besides, I'll stay and thank you for it." An audible sigh went up from the crew. "Though I will miss the Serpent and her crew. You've treated me as well as I could've hoped for."

"Remember us to the merchants, then," winked the captain, and he strode confidently down the gangplank and onto the wharf below.

Jim Quartermaster cleared his throat. "Your pay, Sunchaser." He handed her a purse that was heftier than she'd expected. "Plus a little from the crew." Unsure what else to do, she thanked him and tied it to her belt where the one she'd lost had sat. It felt strange there.

One by one the crew drifted off to their duties. Some took their shore leave, while others began unloading cargo onto the dockside, with the rest milling about the deck on various errands. Soon only Henrick was left.

"Henrick, I—" she began, but he cut her off with a shake of his head.

"I knew weeks ago this life wasn't for you," he said. "You're made for bigger things than the Serpent."

"Doesn't make it any easier to leave," she replied.

"Here, I made you something." He pulled a small carving from his pocket. It was an exact replica of her sunchaser pin carved from the bone of a large creature. The detail was even sharper than the original, and she inhaled sharply when she took it from his hand.

"You made this?" She turned it over, examining both sides closely.

Henrick shrugged. "It's a hobby I learned from Bosun. He says I'm passable."

"This is amazing!" She took a piece of twine from her pack and tied it through one of the gaps at the top of the emblem, then made a loop with one of the knots he'd shown her and hung it around her neck. He'd polished it to such a high shine that when the sun caught it, it sent rays off in every direction. "I'll never forget you, you know."

"Nor I you." He looked down and shuffled his feet, then sniffed and raised his head "Now, it's high time you were off on your next adventure! Got all your things?" Glorya nodded, unable to trust her voice. "Then what are you waiting for? I'll see you to the portmaster's office."

She took his arm, and they strode off into the morning.

JOURNEY OF DUST

Glorya Sunchaser stepped ashore from her latest job, her first few steps faltering slightly as she readjusted to life on land. Over the last year she'd spent most of her time at sea, staying on dry land just long enough to find her next job and grab a few essentials. She'd made enough money to afford some better clothing for working aboard ship: a pair of leather breeches and a finer-spun linen shirt than what she'd worn on her first job, plus a pair of supple leather boots to match. Even lost a bit of weight so it all looks far more dashing, she thought as she strode toward the nearest inn and pub.

A year's travel saw Glorya further south than she'd ever imagined. She'd seen at least eight different ports across multiple countries, some of which she'd barely even heard of, and had honed her skills against stronger storms than she'd ever seen, with exception of her first job on the Serpent and the hurricane she'd overcome. Not a feat I'd like to repeat anytime soon, she thought.

This spring saw her in the port of Joveru, the westernmost port of the country of Zhedaba. It was an arid land, very different from the fertile farming country she'd known most of her life, but the disparity drew her in and piqued her curiosity almost to a fever pitch. The air smelled heavily of spice and the tang of metallurgy as she passed out of the docks and into the commercial area of Joveru, which was made up of a strange combination of merchant stalls, food vendors, and squat buildings that housed more types of metalworking than Glorya could count. These last contained as many windows as security would allow in order to capitalize on the breezes swept off the ocean and across the ultra-hot smithies within. Each had an attached shop where customers could peruse the fruits of the smiths' labors, from heavy ships' anchors to the finest chains and gem-studded pendants. Glorya studiously avoided the jewelry shops in an effort to save as much of her earnings as she could despite the calls from the vendors as she passed. "Such beautiful hair should show off the finest gems in all Zhedaba! Emeralds and sapphires for the lady!"

Glorya caught her reflection in a burnished mirror across the narrow street despite her attempts to avoid the stalls. Her copper hair was pulled back in a few practical braids that were mildly crusted with salt, and the freckles she'd always had across her nose—cursed things—had started to blend together into what might approximate a tan. Her sharp green eyes stood out starkly against the rest of her rounded, soft features, and she realized that she'd lost some more weight as she surveyed her cheekbones. The fit of her clothing confirmed; her breeches were belted as tight as they would go, and while her shirt fit comfortably in the chest, it billowed around her waist. Still have those hips, though. Never getting rid of those. At least they were stronger than they once were. Her boots, thankfully, still fit perfectly. I need a bath, she thought, frowning at her reflection.

The stall's owner caught her woolgathering and took the opportunity to pitch his wares. "Fine mirrors for the lady! See our pocket mirrors!"

"Not today," she replied, "but I could use an inn if you could direct me to one." She produced a coin from the purse under her shirt. After having her old purse stolen in Fisherman's Watch she'd taken to keeping it either inside her belt or between her breasts, depending on the circumstances.

The merchant's eyes shined for a moment and the coin

disappeared into his palm. "Two streets down and left, the finest inn in Joveru! Far enough from the smithies you won't smell them. Run by my cousin, Juma. Tell her Romu sent you." He flipped back the sleeves on his voluminous robes and made a hand gesture Glorya had never seen before.

"Thank you," she replied, nodding, and headed in the direction of the inn.

True to the merchant's word, the inn appeared around a corner not far from the stalls. It looked clean and well cared for, so Glorya entered and surveyed the interior, finding it largely a match for the outside: plain and nondescript, but scrupulously clean and neatly arranged. The walls inside and out were whitewashed, which lent itself to a well-lit dining space with efficiently placed tables throughout. The unoccupied chairs were pushed in and small arrangements of decorative stones and cloth adorned the centers of the tables, each one slightly different from the next. Given the time of day there were few people about, but two or three tables already had occupants.

An amply-proportioned woman with olive skin festooned with chains and rings appeared from behind a swinging door. "Welcome! Welcome! Please, sit down wherever you like." Glorya did her best not to stare as she chose a table in the middle of the room close to the other guests and facing the door. The woman—Juma?—was wearing very little outside of her intricately-draped chains. A cloth of some sort was tied or secured somehow around her hips to cover what was prudent for cleanliness, but her chest and legs were bare, and she bore piercings through which she'd threaded fine chains and dangling jewels. The overall effect was of constant movement and gentle tinkling every time she spoke. She approached Glorya's table and made another hand gesture Glorya did not recognize. "Can I get you something to eat? Drink? Accommodations for the night?" Her speech was accented, but highly intelligible.

Meeting the woman's eyes—and only her eyes—Glorya asked absently what her hostess would recommend. Her eyes twinkled as she replied, "Our special today is a baked white fish with spices and a side of fried gourds." Glorya thanked the hostess and said that would be fine. The woman swept back through the swinging door into what was presumably the kitchen, humming quietly as she went.

Now that she was past the initial shock, Glorya took stock of the rest of the room's occupants. Two, a man and a woman at separate tables, wore similar attire to the hostess's, though neither had as many chains and jewels about their person, while the last was a man who looked like a dockworker from any given port Glorya had visited. She had run across Zhcdabans before, but always as deckhands or crew on the ships on which she served, and never without the voluminous coverings they seemed to prefer. Many chose to either bind their robes closer to their person while working aboard ships or adopted breeches and tunics out of concerns for their safety. She'd never talked to any of them about their home ports or culture. Knowledge that would come in handy right now.

Before long the hostess reappeared with her food. "Fish with fried gourds," she announced as she placed the plate in front of Glorya. "Can I get you a glass of wine to accompany it?"

This time Glorya managed to relax far enough to find her manners. "Wine would be lovely, thank you, as long as it's not too hard on the purse." She even managed a smile.

Her hostess winked conspiratorially. "I know just the thing." She quoted a price that was quite reasonable, then strode to a rack at the back of the room and uncorked a bottle that was sitting on the table before it, pouring a glass for Glorya and filling a second besides. "Do you mind if I sit?" she asked, gesturing to the chair to Glorya's left. Mouth full, Glorya gestured for her to be welcome.

The woman sat heavily, as if she had been on her feet for some time, and took a generous sip from her glass. "I am Juma," she began, nodding slightly and making another of the hand gestures Glorya was coming to associate with some mode of communication of which she wasn't aware. "If you do not mind my forwardness, it seems you have not spent much time in Joveru...or any other part of Zhedaba."

Glorya swallowed hurriedly and replied, "Nice to meet you, Juma. I'm Glorya, and no, I have not; this is my first trip into Joveru." She paused to take another mouthful of the fried gourd, which she had to admit was quite delicious. Fish was something she'd had plenty of in many forms, and while this fish was good, it was more of a known quantity for her despite the difference in seasoning.

Juma nodded, the chains and dangling jewels on her ears and nose tinkling gently. "Please forgive my forwardness—I am forever lost in the nuances of a language that is entirely spoken, with so little context. I wish to give you what your people call 'advice,' if you are willing to hear it." She paused to sip her wine and wait for Glorya's response. Her eyes continually strayed to Glorya's hands and arms as they spoke, which seemed odd to Glorya; she was used to direct eye contact as the best way to reassure someone she was listening.

"I would be most grateful," she replied. "I have worked with Zhedabans aboard ships, but I know very little of the culture here, and I fear a misstep. It's very different from my home."

"I am very glad to be of service, then! Where to start, where to start…" Juma's hands strayed to her chains in half-thought-out gestures or distracted fiddling. "Ah, my hands have led me to the answer." She smiled and indicated her adornments. "As you can see, our indoor mode of dress is not what you are used to. In Zhedaba, it is considered polite to leave as little of the body covered as possible when not out of doors. Cleanliness is, of course, a concern, but as you can see we have standards for that in public places. In one's home is another story entirely. The reason for this is that clothes muddy our communication, which is done through a combination of words and gestures." She set down her nearly-empty wine glass and stood. "Watch." Sidling over to the next table, Juma spoke to the Zhedaban man seated nearby, who had finished his meal. The two exchanged multiple gestures and few words, and she took his empty plate back to the kitchen before rejoining Glorya. "Words are to get attention; the body is to communicate intent and meaning. We have separate gestures for outdoors, where we must hide our bodies from the withering sun."

As she finished her meal, Glorya thought back on the Zhedaban deckhands she'd worked with and realized that they spoke very little, even when addressed, but always seemed to coordinate their activities well amongst each other. Perhaps there is something to having nonverbal communication to use while working aboard a ship.

"I see you are a thoughtful one," Juma mused, cocking her head to one side.

"I'm considering the few Zhedabans I've worked with," Glorya responded. "Do you have any recommendations for finding work aboard Zhedaban ships? I usually pass from port to port and find work with the portmaster as I go, and I've just finished a job."

Juma pursed her lips in thought. "It depends on your skills. Most Zhedaban ships will hire crew with little regard for nationality, though you should exercise caution when accepting work; our laws extend only to those who practice our ways, so less reputable merchants will stiff you on pay or give you the hardest chores." She surveyed Glorya's attire and build appraisingly. "You appear to be no stranger to hard work, though it is difficult for me to judge with so much cloth in the way. Please forgive me if I judge incorrectly."

"No, you are correct; I was raised on a farm, and assist with deck work when it's needed aboard whatever ship I join. But my main skill is keeping the weather calm."

Juma's eyebrows shot upward. "Is that the meaning of your pin?" She gestured broadly toward the golden sun pinned to Glorya's shirt. Glorya nodded, and Juma continued. "Such skills are not common among our people, and are only desired along the coast; in the desert, we have no need for more sun. You should find plenty of work in Joveru." Juma stood gracefully and made a gesture that resembled a bow. "If you would like, I have rooms available for however long you wish to stay. My rates are slightly higher than some, but you will find you are not disturbed in my establishment. Please see me or any of my staff if you wish to rent a room. The staff wear roses on their chests, like mine." She indicated a jeweled red flower just above her left nipple.

"Thank you, I think I will," Glorya responded as she wiped her mouth on the cloth napkin provided and stood. "You've been most helpful." They negotiated a rate for her stay, and she included a small gratuity in her first night's payment. Juma thanked her, and with a twinkle in her eye, replied, "I think you will do just fine in Joveru." She cleared the table they'd shared and swept into the kitchen.

Glorya looked at the oddly-shaped key she'd been given. It had a paddle-shaped handle bearing the image of a sun, and as she reached the top of the stairs she realized each room had a different picture painted brightly on the door. At the end of the hall was a door that matched the image on her key, so she tried the lock. It opened silently, the door swinging open on whispering hinges.

The room beyond was plain, but clean, with white-washed walls and comfortable furnishings. It contained a bed with a soft-looking mattress and crisp sheets, a bench or stool made of wicker, and a three-legged bedside table. Setting her pack down beside the bed, Glorya sank down onto the stool and leaned against the wall. First things first: I need a bath.

A few coins and a slightly salty bath later, Glorya had changed into her spare set of clothing and hung up her freshly-washed work clothes to dry. It was mid-afternoon, but she hadn't slept much or well over the last few weeks, and she decided to spend the rest of the afternoon going through her things, assessing what she needed while in port, and writing a letter to her parents. She wasn't quite sure when she'd get a chance to send it, but better to have it done when the chance arose.

After a delicious dinner in a more crowded common

room than earlier in the day, Glorya found herself weaving up the stairs to her room, exhausted. She collapsed into bed as the sun sank beneath the heat-streaked horizon.

The next dawn saw Glorya winding her way through the streets of Joveru, pack slung over one shoulder, in search of the portmaster. She had to traverse a good portion of what appeared to be the merchants' quarter to reach the docks, and it was busier than she'd expected it to be; most port towns didn't start business until well after sunup. Here she saw men and women animatedly gesticulating over wares, delivering heaping carts of brightly-colored cloth, and exchanging gleaming gemstones for coins or other wares. Most wore loose robes in a blinding palette of colors, producing payment and storing purchases within their folds in a myriad of ways.

By the time the sun cleared the horizon she'd found what appeared to be the portmaster's office. The early sun streamed through a set of windows on the east side of the building, illuminating a whipcord-thin man within. He was dressed as any Zhedaban man would be indoors, though with a slightly larger cloth about his loins and buttocks, perhaps out of deference to the two foreign sailors with whom he was doing business. Both other men seemed ill at ease; their attire marked them as from off the continent, closer to Glorya's homeland than to Zhedaba. They handed the portmaster their manifests, then hurried out of the office, almost bowling Glorya over in their rush. Raising an eyebrow, she entered the building in their wake.

The portmaster was younger than she'd expected and regarded her for a moment before addressing her. His accent was thick, but not unpleasant, and she was still very much able to understand him. "Name and vessel, and I'll need your manifests."

"Glorya Sunchaser, at your service, sir," she replied, watching the man's eyebrows rise and his gaze fall to the pin on her shirt. "I'm looking for work."

"I'll say you are," he replied, seating himself behind a modest desk and motioning for her to join him. "What sort of vessel? Any preference for route?" He opened a book and began to scribble in it, the letters and numbers foreign to her.

"I'd prefer a larger merchant vessel if there's one in port. Longer routes make for better pay, especially those that cross the straits, but I'll take any you have that are trustworthy." The man looked up sharply, his gaze narrowing slightly, and he nodded.

"You're wise to ask about trustworthiness. We have a fair few come in that would rule out. As it stands, you're in luck; the Tezhu is in port, and their route usually takes them south around the cape. The weather is strong down there, and the journey takes months, but the trade is rich that way. You'll find them on the center dock, in the…" he consulted the book before him for a moment, "third bay on the right."

"My thanks," Glorya said, inclining her head, and strode confidently toward the docks.

The Tezhu soared regally a full half mast above the rest of the vessels moored at the center—and largest—of Joveru's three main docks. It was a two-masted deep-sea vessel with a shallow, elongated quarterdeck and strangely-hung white sails. Going to have to relearn sail work and rigging to help there, Glorya thought as she surveyed the configuration of ropes connected to the sails. The outer hull was painted a deep green with the exception of the figurehead, which was a lifelike rendition of a red-haired, tanned mermaid. Glorya rolled her eyes at the thought of the jokes she was likely to hear, then took up a spot next to the gangplank to wait for a crew member to pass.

Before long a man in rough, brown robes approached the gangplank carrying a large barrel on one shoulder. "Excuse me," Glorya began, then stopped as the man made a gesture with his free hand—palm turned down, hand moving outward away from his body—and kept walking. Glorya's brow furrowed. *Maybe he doesn't understand, or can't help me. I'll ask the next person.* She didn't have long to wait before a woman approached with a large basket on her head. "Excuse m—" Glorya didn't even finish her phrase before the woman steadied her basket with one hand, then made the same gesture and continued up the gangplank.

A small hand tugged at her shirt tail. Looking down, Glorya was greeted by the open face of a small girl dressed in flowing, orange robes. "I can help you," she said as soon as she was acknowledged, and held out a hand. Glorya raised an eyebrow, then produced a coin from her purse, placing it into the upturned palm, where it took up most of the available real estate. The coin disappeared before she could blink and the girl put a hand to the top of her chest, then moved it out toward Glorya. "They cannot answer you while they are working. It is our custom not to stop while we have a task to do. The gesture they are making is polite apology. I know your people do not talk with their hands, as we do, so this would not make sense to you." She made the same gesture both workers had made as they had passed.

"Then how am I supposed to find someone who can tell

me if they're hiring?" Glorya asked the diminutive figure.

"They will find you. One of the workers who apologized will tell bosun and they will come see you when they are free. May...may I touch your hair?" The girl made the polite apology gesture as she asked, nearly in the same breath as her statement.

Glorya smiled. "If you tell me what this meant." She copied the girl's hand-to-chest gesture as she bent down.

"It is thank you." The girl reached a tentative hand toward Glorya's braids, gently running her fingers over the bumps. "So beautiful...I have only heard stories of the flame hair." She withdrew her hand with a sigh. "I should go. When bosun comes, do this." The girl stood up stock straight and placed a fist over her opposite shoulder. "It shows respect for people who make rules on ships."

Glorya answered by copying the thank-you gesture and was rewarded with a grin from the girl before she sped off down the dock to rejoin a woman who was leaving one of the fish stalls nearby. The woman bent over to listen to the girl's excited words, then looked back toward Glorya, who smiled in return.

She spent the next hour watching deck hands come and go from the Tezhu carrying all manner of barrels, crates, boxes, and bags. Strange smells wafted from some, while others appeared unusually heavy. Glorya kept one eye on the tide, concerned the vessel would be ready to leave before anyone appeared to ask about employment.

Just then she noticed the deckhands stop their work, saluting just as the girl had shown Glorya that morning as a woman strode down the gangplank. Seeing her opportunity, Glorya placed a fist over her shoulder and stood as tall as she could as the woman passed.

Her robes were an exact match for the color of the

ship's outer hull. The hood was thrown back, revealing strong, weathered features and salt-and-pepper hair with steel-gray streaks at the temples and forehead. Her flinty gaze passed over Glorya, then snapped back to her as she stepped off the gangplank. "At ease," she said, and Glorya relaxed slightly, letting her arm drop to her side. "You seek work. What is your skill?"

"Sunchaser and deckhand, ma'am," Glorya replied, meeting the woman's gaze. A fleeting expression of distaste washed over the woman's face, then was banished as she replied.

"We may have need of your services on our trip. You can also serve on deck?"

Glorya nodded. "I'm comfortable in the rigging, too, but will need to learn your ships first. I'm used to more... northern trading vessels."

"Good. Can you work with one who calls the wind?"

The question took Glorya aback. *They taught us in school, but we didn't do much practice...* "I know the way of it," she replied warily.

"Then we can use you." They discussed pay, settled on an amount—everyone here seemed to haggle over anything they possibly could—and Glorya was given permission to go aboard.

Most of the preparations to get under way had been completed, so Glorya had little trouble finding a deckhand without occupation to ask directions. Most barely spoke her language, and she realized belatedly she didn't see a single non-Zhedaban crewmate aboard. *Looks like I'll have to pay a lot more attention and start learning a new language, gestures and all.* She eventually made her way to a mid-level crewman who spoke her language fluently and was able to show her where to stow her pack.

The crew's quarters were similar to every other set of berths she'd acclimated to over the last year. At least that's familiar, she thought as she placed her pack inside the chest beneath her bunk and went in search of the crewman who'd helped her.

Glorya had just found employment splicing ropes when the on-deck crew stood to attention facing the gangplank. Joining them, she watched as the woman who had hired her and another Zhedaban in matching green, a woman with an ornate hood over her head, strode up the gang-plank and onto the shallow quarterdeck. Both turned as a third woman, long of limb and fine of feature, made her leisurely way up the gangplank behind them. Her ombre hood was thrown back, revealing light olive skin and long, black hair in a ponytail atop her head. Jeweled chains ran from her ponytail down to piercings in her ears, then to her nose, then down to her neck, dripping precious stones as it ran beneath her multicolored robes. She barely noted the presence of the deckhands as she sashayed up the steps and onto the quarterdeck to join the other two women.

Glorya looked questioningly at the crewman next to her. He leaned over and whispered, "Wind caller Gilena. Hired yesterday for our journey."

So that's who I'll be working with, Glorya thought. Should be interesting; she has the look of a noblewoman. Wonder how she'll do on a ship.

Without a word spoken aloud the crew returned to work with even more fervor than before. Within fifteen minutes they were ready to cast off, just making the tide as it left the bay. Glorya watched as the strangely-hung sails unfurled into triangular swaths of white cloth covered in intricate golden threadwork. As the sun caught the patterns in the sails they gleamed and returned its rays in an opulent display of dancing sunlight. She had to admit the effect was impressive.

The wooden bars attached to the sails and masts swivelled as a stiff wind swept across the deck from bowsprit to fantail. Glorya looked up from her splicing in time to see it pick up Gilena's ponytail and send it streaming behind her as she held her face upturned to the sky, arms raised. Closing her eyes, Glorya watched with her inner senses as Gilena directed the wind up from the deck and filled the sails, pushing the ship slowly away from the dock. At least she knows what she's about, Glorya thought as she went back to her mending.

They cleared the port and the bay quickly and deftly, and before Glorya knew it they'd left Joveru behind to sink slowly below the horizon. Gilena withdrew once they were in open water, making her way slowly down the quarterdeck and into the cabins beneath. Glorya thought she saw the woman falter slightly as she took her first step downward. Maybe I'm imagining things, or maybe that exhausted her. She made a mental note to keep an eye on the woman, either way.

The first week out from port was uneventful. Glorya found a few more crew who were able to speak with her and began learning more about the ship's rigging and sail workings. It was fascinating; the Tezhu, despite its size, could tack more easily and maneuver more deftly than many of the smaller vessels on which she'd worked. Its crew was larger than she'd realized and showed a level of coordination she wouldn't have thought possible with so many people involved. The secret seemed to be in the motions and hand gestures the crew used to communicate across the deck. It was eerily quiet topside, but there was always a wealth of communication going between the crew, as she was gradually learning.

The woman who had hired Glorya turned out to be the bosun, as she'd expected, and she ran a very tight ship. They'd only spoken once more in the week they'd been at sea, and then only when she'd asked Glorya to check on a few clouds the crew had noticed. She didn't seem the kind of person of whom anyone wished to run afoul. The captain was equally taciturn and allowed the bosun to run most of the ship's daily activities, only surfacing from her cabin long enough to navigate the ship. Gilena often joined her in her cabin if she was not needed to steer the winds, leaving Glorya to wonder exactly what their relationship was. Not that it's my business, she reminded herself as she went about her chores.

At the start of the second week out from port Glorya noticed a bruise on the horizon. Reaching out with her senses, she determined they were headed directly for a large weather system that could possibly cause them days of difficulty if it wasn't taken care of. She'd studied systems around this side of the world, and it seemed most of them stayed over the water, or didn't go far inland, meaning she could dismantle it without affecting farming or overall weather patterns elsewhere. These were cyclical storms, and another would take its place in a matter of weeks, at most, bringing rain where it was needed.

She notified the bosun, who nodded in response to her request to take up a spot in the rigging and handle the storms. As she headed for the mainmast, a deckhand slipped quietly into the captain's cabin, unnoticed by the crew. Glorya took up her usual spot, twisted her feet into the ropes, and made herself as comfortable as she could.

Her senses told her this was a widespread formation. Thankfully, no single portion of it was terribly strong, but taken in totality the system was concerning. Glorya reached out, eyes closed, and began to find the keys to dismantling it before they came too close. She'd spent the last year training herself to work across ever-growing distances and as a result was fairly confident she could handle this one before they felt so much as a gentle rocking of the deck.

"May I be of assistance...Sunchaser?" The voice cut through her concentration, surprising her; most sounds had little effect. It seemed to resonate through both her physical and metaphysical senses with a sonorous tone.

Glorya glanced down at the deck. Gilena waited there, a look of mild distaste on her finely-wrought features as she awaited a response. "Thank you, but I think I can handle this system before it becomes an issue. If you do feel the winds getting out of control, I would thank you to redirect them before they blow us off course in case I'm wrong."

Gilena shrugged to hide the smallest of eye rolls. "As you wish." Instead of returning to the captain's cabin, she headed up to the quarterdeck to watch. You won't pressure me, Glorya thought as she closed her eyes and returned to her work. Just you try.

For the first few minutes, everything went smoothly. The closest groups of clouds melted apart as she reached into their sources and systematically split apart the ties binding them together. Glorya relaxed into her work, enjoying the simple effectiveness of it. About halfway through the system something began to tug harder at her attempts to calm the storms. The clouds were dispersing, but not the direction or way she expected them to; every time she split them apart, they would make a circle and blow back together to re-form. Strange; I don't recall sensing winds aloft. She shifted her attention to the winds instead—and met resistance. The harder she tried to quell them, the stronger they blew, until she realized the storm was strengthening again instead of dispersing. Odd; I've never seen a system act this way before. So she shifted her attention back to dispersing the clouds and reducing the strength of the storm itself.

Glorya lost track of time while she was weatherworking, and before the storm was halfway navigable she began to tire. Opening her eyes, she looked around to anchor herself back on the ship. The crew largely kept their distance while she was working, and this was no exception; they gave her a wide berth as she climbed down and mounted the steps onto the quarterdeck to update the bosun. Gilena was still at the rear of the quarterdeck watching the storm approach.

"I am having unexpected difficulty in dispersing this storm," Glorya told the bosun, who stood beside the helmsman.

The woman frowned. "Is it beyond your skill?"

"It shouldn't be, by all appearances," Glorya replied, letting her frustration show in her expression. "I've quelled far larger in a shorter time frame. Something is fighting me."

"Perhaps Gilena can help." The bosun made a gesture and turned to face the other weatherworker, who stood lazily from her posture leaning on the railing and joined them.

"You called?" she asked with a smug expression.

"The sunchaser is having difficulty with this storm. I request that you work together for the protection of the crew and ship," the bosun replied in a slightly more terse manner than usual. Seems she doesn't like this Gilena any more than I do, Glorya thought.

Gilena nodded and turned to Glorya. "How may I be of assistance?" She raised a carefully-manicured eyebrow.

"The winds are fighting my attempts to disperse them," Glorya explained. A fleeting expression she couldn't name crossed Gilena's face—triumph?—before disappearing in her response.

"I can direct them if it will assist you."

"Can you keep them from pushing the clouds together? I can do the rest if I don't have to fight the clouds re-forming constantly."

"Of course...Sunchaser," Gilena replied with a slight smirk. Glorya ignored it and took up a spot at the railing on the quarterdeck, closing her eyes and continuing her work. She felt better after the short break and was confident it wouldn't take much longer to disassemble the storms with a bit of assistance.

At first, it seemed to be working; she could feel Gilena directing the winds in seemingly random directions, which helped keep the clouds from forming into groups as quickly. Glorya found she could almost "see" the link between Gilena's influence and the winds' movements and took a moment to watch in fascination. Gilena was very deft in her manipulation of the air within the storm; she seemed to enjoy picking the winds apart into the tiniest wisps and watching them weave intricate patterns. Glorya took a moment to appreciate her skill before going back to her task of pulling apart the pieces of the system as a whole.

Before long Glorya became slowly aware of a tickling sensation on the back of her neck as the small hairs that fell out of her braid were lifted by a breeze. Opening her eyes momentarily she saw that the wind had picked up across the deck and was starting to shift the ship's course. What am I missing? she thought as she cast her senses back into the storm. All she could see for a moment was where she'd left off pulling apart the storm...but suddenly the idea occurred to her to rotate her perspective. As her "sight" shifted she realized the intricate weaving she'd been watching had been moving the storm closer and closer to the ship. I'm out of time.

"Gilena...the winds..." Glorya shouted to be heard over the sudden gale. "They're pushing toward us, not away. I need you to move them to buy us time!"

"Thought...you could handle it..." Gilena replied breathlessly.

"Not if I'm fighting you, too," Glorya answered, leaning onto the railing. She could feel her strength draining.

The bosun's head snapped around at this last exchange, transfixing Gilena with a stare. "Does she speak truth? Are you working against the sunchaser?"

Gilena didn't reply, instead sagging toward the railing. A trickle of blood escaped from her nose and ran down her perfectly-painted lips, staining a path to her chin. Leaning on her elbows, she let a drop fall onto the wood before slumping onto the quarterdeck, unconscious.

Glorya barely registered the windwaker's impact on the boards, instead refocusing her attention on the imminent storm. "I'll do what I can, but it won't be enough," she shouted to the bosun, who nodded and took the wheel, making some pointed hand gestures to various crew members around the boat.

After that Glorya lost herself in the storm. She knew she didn't have a chance at dispersing it, but she could

lessen the impact and give them a chance to make it closer
to land if she could just figure out which pieces to take
apart. The winds were a tangled mess after Gilena's inter-
vention, so she started by picking them apart one strand
at a time, then moved on to the nearest clouds. At some
point it registered that her elbows were starting to hurt as
they dug into the quarterdeck railing, but she pushed the
sensation aside and threw herself further into the storm.
No time for pain. Lives at stake, including my own. She
thought she managed to get the immediate area around
the ship calmed enough for steering to be possible, but by
the time she heard a surprised shout and "Brace yourself!"
from the bosun, Glorya was so absorbed in her work she
didn't have the time or energy to do much besides fall
bonelessly to the deck when they ran aground.

Glorya's sense of touch awakened first. Her clothes
were soaked through and had the slightly itchy feeling she
associated with sea water, not rain. Smell woke up shortly
after and bombarded her with salty spray and seaweed.
The sand beneath her face told her she was no longer
aboard the Tezhu, and by the time she was able to open
her eyes she'd deduced through fuzzy thoughts that they
had run aground in the storm. Some help I was.

Pushing herself up, Glorya looked around. Much of the
crew appeared to be present; the bosun was directing them
in removing items from the ship before the tide took it
back out into the sea to its final resting place. Neither the
captain nor Gilena seemed to have made an appearance.
Shrugging, Glorya approached the bosun to see how she
could help.

The Tezhu's hull was beached in the rough surf about
waist deep in waters still tossed by the rough weather. It

was raining lightly to boot, and many of the crew were having trouble getting to and from the ship due to the heavy undertow. They went in pairs to help each other unload as much cargo as they could carry, a few also carrying bags of personal items. Glorya paired up with a man roughly her size and began helping unload. Thankfully her pack had survived where she'd stowed it under her bunk, and she retrieved it on the first trip back to the ship. At some point it occurred to her to see if Gilena was still slumped on the quarterdeck, but it was empty. Perhaps they already moved her, Glorya thought with a sinking feeling in her gut.

Before long the tide began to turn and the undertow was too great to safely make it to the ship. The bosun called the crew together and spoke briefly, exchanging many hand gestures with the crew, then approached Glorya as the rain stopped. "We will stay here for the night and make ready to travel in the morning. It is now afternoon, which gives us little time. Based on our course it is closer to go inland to the hills where our people mine the earth, taking with us as much as we can for trade. You will be able to find passage back to Joveru there, or to our capital city. Either will get you back to your people."

"Bosun, if you please, I was wondering what happened to Gilena. She was not on the deck when I went to look."

The bosun scowled. "By the time the ship ran aground she had fallen overboard. The sea knew the fate she deserved."

"What about the captain?" Glorya asked as she processed this last.

"She was lost trying to save her lover from going overboard. They are together, at least." The bosun turned and beckoned for Glorya to follow. "I find it strange to be called 'Bosun,' though that is your people's word for my task; please, call me Veda." She led Glorya to the larger of a few groups of crew members, which was clustered around what looked to be some sort of desert-going contraption. "We will use this to carry cargo and supplies across the dunes to the mines, where many of our families work." She exchanged a few unintelligible words with the person in charge of repairing the strange-looking carriage, which had been damaged in the wreck, then motioned for Glorya to follow her over to a stack of crates. "In the meantime, you and I will speak of our culture and how to get you safely home." Veda opened one of the crates, digging through for a moment before producing a dark green robe similar to the one she herself wore. It was barely more than a large, rectangular piece of cloth, but was miraculously dry, unlike Glorya's current attire. "Take off your clothes."

"Here?" Glorya stared for a moment.

"Where else is there?" Veda gestured expansively at the beach. She was right; the only shelter anywhere on the beach was by the large cliffs to their north, which were devoid of anything resembling a cave. Veda shook her head. "Your people are strange; you cover your bodies as if they are all different. Look. I will show you how the robes work." She began unwinding her own robes. They were wound in a surprisingly intricate fashion, and Glorya had trouble following the older woman's motions. Before long she stood on the beach, naked but for a few chains about her waist, holding a large bundle of cloth before her. No one else on the beach took any notice, but Glorya couldn't help blushing. "You see? The cloth keeps the sun from our skin and the lack underneath cools us. If you wear your clothes in the desert, you will die. Now, take off your clothes." She began to re-wind her own robes as Glorya awkwardly shrugged out of her soaked shirt and breeches. "Keep the boots; we have no extra sandals. Now, watch." Veda took the robe she had found for Glorya and began winding it around her, covering every inch of skin and somehow leaving a hood for her to pull up if she desired. The entire process was fascinating enough it almost took Glorya's mind off of being publicly naked for the first time in her life. This is definitely on the list of things I never thought I would do.

"There." Veda tucked in the final corner of the cloth and admired her work. "Much better. You may survive the journey." She re-closed the crate she'd opened and sat down on it. "Please sit."

Glorya found another crate close by and seated herself, awkwardly arranging her robes so that she was comfortable. She had to admit it was very freeing not to have the constraints of breeches. "How can I help?" she asked. "I feel responsible for what happened."

Veda made the gesture Glorya had learned to mean "no," only with more force. "You were true to your word and self. It was Gilena who doomed us all. Do not carry her guilt with you; there will be enough to carry as it is.

"But let us talk of you. First, it is obvious you are not Zhedaban." Glorya touched her hair reflexively, looking down at herself. "If you can learn enough of our ways, maybe some of our speech, you will be accepted when we reach the hills. They are not as...approving of outsiders as the port towns. It will also be necessary to hide what you are." Veda nodded toward the golden pin on Glorya's rumpled shirt next to them on the sand. "That needs to be set aside for the time being. Your name, also, is hard for our people; we will find you a new one to use while you travel with us. Our names are short because they show our importance in relation to the things around us. Gilena was an exception because she worked the winds, and her kind are sacred among us. Your kind…" she made a complicated gesture, then shrugged awkwardly. "There are not many like you among our people, and the ones we have die young. Most try to take on the sandstorms and do not live to tell of it. Do not make their mistake." She stood, motioning for Glorya to follow her again. "For now you will be called Lori; it is close to your foreign name, but short enough for Zhedaba." She didn't wait for Glorya's response before continuing toward another group.

A year away from school and I'm back to studying, Glorya thought as she followed Veda. I have a lot to learn, and little time in which to do it.

Before long Veda had made Glorya's introductions to the group, explaining that only a few of them spoke bits and pieces of her language. "They will help you learn our ways," Veda explained. "It is best to learn when forced to use what you are learning. Mavu will help you get settled for the night, then find you work in the morning. Sleep well." With that, she trotted off to help the team fixing the carriage-contraption.

Glorya found herself staring at a ring of unfamiliar faces. All seemed to be former deckhands; she'd seen most of them in passing over the past week, but had never had reason to speak with them, or any real way to communicate with them. Now they were to be her lifeline crossing the desert. May as well get started. "Hello," she ventured, waving slightly. The group blinked at her, almost as one.

None of them spoke, but the oldest woman stepped forward, arm extended at head height, palm facing out, wrinkled fingers held close together. The rest followed suit.

Glorya took this as her first lesson and copied the gesture. The woman reached out and moved her hand down slightly, her touch firm, but maternally gentle. Taking the hint, Glorya made a mental note and practiced one more time. The woman nodded, then waved for Glorya to follow. At least that's the same, she thought.

They camped for the night directly on the beach under the stars. The ship had been carrying a good amount of cloth as cargo, so there were plenty of blankets; it was colder than Glorya would have expected, especially on the coast of the hottest place she'd visited. The sand was uncomfortable, but she found that if she shaped it to her body she was able to get comfortable enough, and with as much weatherworking as she'd done that day she was completely exhausted. As soon as she was settled, she was asleep.

They rose before dawn the next morning. The team that had been working on the carriage-contraption had finished sometime in the night, and the group loaded as many supplies as they could into its bed and onto the single trailer connected to it before taking up the long runners attached to the front and heading into the desert.

Glorya's designated group walked behind the trailer, waiting for their turn to pull. They exchanged few words, but the woman who had taught Glorya the greeting last night walked beside her, teaching her gestures as they went. Before their midmorning stop she had learned how to introduce herself and how to agree and disagree with something someone said. So far they had used very few words she understood; the woman, Mavu, spoke very little of Glorya's language. The rest of the group seemed to follow her implicitly, and Glorya wondered if it was out of respect for her age and experience or some other inducement. She decided to observe the other groups to see if she could determine any sort of definitive social structure.

While they were stopped, Veda approached. Glorya greeted her with the hand signal she'd learned, and Veda smiled with one corner of her mouth. "You are learning from Mavu. Good. While we are stopped, rest and drink. The desert drains a body of its water faster than the sea." She handed Glorya what might have been a gourd that was filled with water. Glorya took a deep draught, then handed it back, making the "thank you" gesture. Veda responded with another gesture, the reverse of the one Glorya had made. That must be "you're welcome," she thought, and filed it away for future use.

They continued on for a few hours, trading out teams to pull the carriage every hour or so. The further inland they drew, the hotter it became, and the faster they had to change teams. Eventually the sun reached its zenith and they stopped, erecting a shade that used the cart as its main support. Mavu made the "good night" gesture Glorya had seen her use before going to sleep the previous night and folded herself down onto the sand in the shade of the cart. I hope to be that limber at her age, Glorya thought as she watched the older woman nod off. Many of the other crew were doing the same, and Glorya took the hint, finding herself more tired than she'd expected. Walking in the heat—especially while pulling the cart—was exhausting, and she found it easier to fall asleep than she'd thought.

Before long she was roused by another from her group, a man about her height and slight of build. He beckoned her to follow and showed her how to dismantle the shade from the cart. She learned the signs for left, right, above, and below and committed them to memory as they took another turn pulling the supplies.

While they pulled Glorya's companions taught her spoken words. She was confused from the start when they tried to teach her their words for sand; they had different words for different kinds, and it wasn't immediately obvious to her how to tell them apart. Mavu made a suggestion and they began naming the items around them, like tigi, which was their name for the robes they wore. The language itself was easy to pronounce and used a very predictable syllabary, so before she knew it Glorya was picking up snippets of conversation from the people around her.

By the second day she had made the habit of watching both faces and hands as people talked. Glorya's travel companions were patient with her forays into using what she'd learned and corrected gently and encouragingly. As the first week ended Glorya realized that she was starting to intuitively comprehend what she was told and was replying confidently, albeit simply, in kind.

Veda visited her for the first time in days as the group made camp for the coldest part of the night. They'd been traveling only between midafternoon and midnight, then before sunup to noon, sleeping during the long breaks and eating as they walked. "How are you holding up?" Veda asked.

Glorya replied with the gesture for well (politely), smiling slightly. Veda beamed. "I see you are learning as fast as I thought you would. Keep going. How was the weather today?" The question was a combination of speech and gesture, ending with the cocked head that denoted a question.

"Warm and sunny with little wind," Glorya replied.

"Good," Veda answered. She drilled Glorya for the next half hour on what she'd learned, correcting where necessary and adding context to a few of the phrases she'd learned by rote but that made little sense or had no direct translation. When she was satisfied, she bade Glorya good night. *I suppose I've made a good impression,* she thought as she set her head on her pack to rest.

Another week of travel—and nearly the end of their supplies—saw the group approaching a large set of bare stone hills. Unlike the mountains near Glorya's home there were no scrub bushes or trees dotting the landscape; these were wind-worn mounds of rock rubbed smooth by millennia of sandblasting. Mavu smiled as the hills came into view.

"Almost there—we will meet family," she told Glorya, her expression conveying what her words did not. This place was home, and she hadn't seen it in a long time.

Veda approached not long after the hills were spotted. "We must talk. I will teach you how to be polite, and you will need to understand more about our ways indoors." Glorya had become comfortable swapping between Zhedaban and her native tongue, even with the addition of gestures to add meaning to the familiar words. She found that sometimes blending the languages could even convey her points better than either alone, which was fascinating to her.

As they walked, Veda explained the next layer of their culture to Glorya. "We have different rules for indoors and out," she began. "We cannot uncover our skin in the sun, but as soon as we are settled inside we disrobe. Homes and businesses have hooks by the door for hanging your tigi. It is very insulting to leave one's tigi on while in a dwelling or meeting place as it shows lack of trust in your host." Veda looked sidelong at Glorya to judge her reaction. "I understand this is strange for your people."

Glorya nodded slowly. "It is, but I am beginning to understand the reasoning behind a lot of Zhedaban culture, and while it is very different from my own, it makes a different kind of sense. I have nothing to hide." She shrugged in what she hoped was a reassuring fashion.

"Good. I would still warn you that you will...stick out among our people. Lighter skin is prized among us, but none are quite so pale, and flame hair is unheard of. Traders from outside do not often visit the hills, either, so you may gather stares. But you will have no shortage of offers for bedmates, should you desire one." Glorya's step faltered for a moment at this last, and Veda chuckled. "We are very open about our relationships as well, you will find. It is fine to decline offers politely if you are not comfortable and no one will think less of you." Glorya nodded as she blushed furiously. This should be an interesting trip.

They pushed through the afternoon rest stop in order to arrive at the hills by nightfall. Food was in short supply, and they needed to make the best time possible so they would not have to camp without dinner. Glorya began to see cart trails heading into a gap between two of the outlying ground swells and realized there was an opening wide enough for two carts of the size they pulled that led directly into a well-lit cave. The sun had almost set, and the cheery light of the torches at the entrance was a welcome sight.

Pulling the cart into the tunnel, Glorya saw that there were large bays hewn into the rock not far from the entrance before various smaller tunnels split off and headed downward. Veda chose a bay for their cart after checking the markings carved into the wall to the left of the opening. There were no obvious security measures, which seemed strange for a storage area, but they left their cargo unattended on the cart and walked wearily toward the smaller tunnels. Mavu appeared at Glorya's elbow. "Lori, follow me. You will stay with my family." Glorya agreed, smiling, and trailed gratefully in the older woman's wake. Mavu seemed to have found a new energy reserve and was moving fast enough Glorya had a hard time keeping up despite her relative youth.

They wound their way through a series of narrowing tunnels deep under the hills that emerged into an expansive central hub. Figures in every color of tigi imaginable bustled about their business, exchanging silent greetings in an undercurrent of communication that gave the room an electric feeling despite the lack of audible exchange. Mavu took Glorya's arm, smiled at her reassuringly, and dove into the mass of humanity headlong.

Glorya lost all sense of direction as they flowed through the river of foot traffic. Mavu seemed to have a destination in mind as she led them haphazardly across the great hall to avoid large groups of people heading in opposing directions. Glorya would have been lost in the press if Mavu hadn't kept a firm grip on her arm. As suddenly as they had entered the chamber they left it, disappearing down another narrow passageway with fewer people. Each of these hallways was barely wide enough for the two of them and their packs to fit through. There must be some system of traffic here; I don't see anyone coming from the other direction, and they couldn't pass if they did. Just then Glorya noticed markings on the walls and tapped Mavu on the arm.

"What does this mean?" She indicated the markings.

"Left only." Mavu confirmed Glorya's theory with two gestures and continued down the hall. "Close now." They arrived at a junction where four hallways converged, two the size and direction of the one Glorya and Mavu were leaving and two larger tunnels that allowed for two-way traffic. They headed down the leftmost of the larger tunnels, which opened into an even wider hallway containing doors on either side. People came and went through the various portals, and Glorya guessed that these were some sort of apartments; each had a different symbol on the door. Sun, cloud, spearhead, is that a flower? She was reminded of the rooms at the inn where she'd stayed in Joveru. I suppose it's a way for them to identify who lives where without surnames. She'd learned on the trip that Zhedaban clans were groups that traveled the desert or worked together moreso than blood relations. Membership in a clan was fluid and could change between jobs or trips, so there were very few concrete groups off of which to base a name.

Mavu stopped outside of a door with an intricately painted geometric design. "My home," she said, grinning from ear to ear, and opened the door.

A wave of sounds and smells hit Glorya as soon as she crossed the threshold. Children ran naked through the main room as they entered, screaming in wordless excitement and hugging Mavu about the knees. She began to unwind her tigi around them, motioning for Glorya to do the same, and hung it on one of a set of pegs just inside the door. Struggling to find the end, Glorya fussed with hers for a few moments, finally finding a starting point and unwinding it bit by bit. Mavu was already wading into the embrace of an older man who bore a striking resemblance to her—her brother, perhaps?—before moving on to the growing line of smiling people waiting to greet her. She turned momentarily toward Glorya, making the gesture Glorya had learned as "guest," and all heads turned as one toward the newcomer.

Glorya froze, her tigi only halfway unwrapped, and began to blush. "Well met," she signed and spoke awkwardly before resuming the battle against her garment. The group blinked at her for a moment, then one of the women about Glorya's age walked forward. She was average height and built like someone accustomed to physical labor, and her dark eyes took in Glorya's red hair with a flash of awe.

"Help?" she asked, venturing a feather-light touch to the corner of Glorya's tigi.

"Please, and thank you," Glorya responded, heaving a sigh of relief. The woman took the loose edge of fabric and within a few short moments had it unwrapped and hanging neatly on the wall. On a peg next to the tigi hung a few small cloths with strings attached, and the woman chose one for Glorya after taking her measure, tying it around her waist to hang just far enough to cover her buttocks. Nodding, she stepped back.

"Minu," the woman introduced herself with an unfamiliar gesture.

"Lori," Glorya replied, using the gesture she'd been taught for introductions. Minu shook her head and repeated the gesture she'd used. Glorya cocked her head in a question, then mimicked Minu's gesture. Minu nodded, then rejoined the group surrounding Mavu.

Mavu was just finishing her greetings as they approached. "Lori, my family," she said, introducing them one by one. There were at least seven present, children not included, and Glorya noticed an obvious resemblance among many of them. She did her best to commit names to memory and responded with the gesture Minu had just taught her, which got her smiles and reassurance all around. All in all, it was enough to set her more at ease despite still acclimating to the fact that everyone around her was mostly naked—including herself.

They moved en masse into another room with a large table, where food sat waiting to be served. Much of it was unfamiliar to Glorya; there was little meat on the table, but the lack was made up with a variety of vegetables and dried substances redolent with spices. A pitcher stood at the end of the table filled with a white, milky substance, condensation beading the outside. Everyone seated themselves in no discernable order on the benches around all four sides of the table and served themselves from the platters of food without preamble. Mavu sat Glorya next to her, then showed her each dish, naming it as it was passed around the table. Most of the names were foreign to her and had no translation, but she tasted everything at least once out of politeness and a deep curiosity, finding it to be heavily spiced and flavorful despite the humble ingredients involved. The milky liquid was made from some of the tubers served as a side dish and was pleasantly chilled with a bright, sweet flavor that complemented the spiced nature of the food.

Glorya ate more than she'd intended to. Conversation flowed around the table in a zephyr that floated past her without her input; it was rapid-fire and used words and gestures she couldn't begin to place. Mavu answered for her a few times, and she caught words and meaning here and there, but for the most part she simply observed how the family interacted. The gestures used at the table were smaller and more nuanced than the ones she'd learned on the trip, but many were similar, and she made a mental note to ask someone if their meanings were the same. She used the ones she knew a few times to answer or ask questions and was not rebuffed, though answers usually came in the form of the smaller gestures she was seeing. Minu was helpful more than once from across the table, making sure to speak and move slowly so that Glorya could follow along.

After dinner everyone helped clear the table and clean the dishes, using sand instead of water to scour them clean and stacking them in neat piles in one corner of the dining room. Glorya made herself useful, glad for the familiar form of interaction, and found her mind wandering back in time to compare her current task with washing pots and pans in the farmhouse kitchen back home. I should tell Mother how well this scrubs, she mused idly as she stacked plates and bowls. Before long the dining room was clean and everyone drifted off to various separate rooms either alone or in small groups. Mavu took Glorya gently by the arm and walked her down a surprisingly long hallway. This is a bigger apartment than I'd thought. At the end was a small, unoccupied room with a mattress and light blanket. "Sleep here tonight," Mavu told her, arranging the blanket. "We will speak in the morning. Sleep well." Smiling, she watched Glorya settle herself gratefully on the mattress and pull up the blanket, then wandered off down the hall.

The tiny room was doorless and was barely big enough to fit the mattress. Glorya couldn't figure out what it was stuffed with; it was too stiff for feathers, but too soft for cotton, and had very small lumps here and there. Still better than sand, Glorya thought as she settled under the homespun blanket. Her last thought before drifting off into a deep slumber was that she could definitely get used to sleeping naked.

Glorya awoke to Minu's gentle touch on her shoulder. "Good morning!" she said enthusiastically. "You have a visitor." She rose from where she knelt on the mattress and waited for Glorya to drag her consciousness into focus, then led her back down the hall to an even smaller room off the same hallway as the bedrooms. Glorya noticed in passing that she was the last one awake. "Bathroom is here," Minu stated, indicating the small room, which contained a very simple hole in the floor. Surprisingly, it didn't smell as bad as Glorya would have expected, and peering down into the hole she realized it wasn't just a hole; there was a definite draft pulling air down into the darkness. Some sort of sewer system? she wondered idly as she used the privy and rejoined Minu.

Veda was waiting at the dining table, sharing a cup of some warm beverage with Mavu. She greeted Glorya, handing her a cup and gesturing for her to sit. Glorya inhaled the steam floating out of her cup and found it to be coffee with spices. Good thing I usually drink it black, she thought as she noticed the distinct lack of cream or dairy products available. Sipping gratefully, she sat and thanked both.

"I have found you passage to Joveru," Veda began once they'd made some small talk to allow Glorya time to fully awaken. "A trade caravan is leaving tomorrow early morning. They will let you travel with them under their clan's protection, which means you should be safe from both bandits and the elements."

"I am in your debt," Glorya replied, breathing a sigh of

relief.

"There is no debt. You saved the lives of much of my crew. Now I have saved yours and will help you find home." Veda tossed back the last of her coffee, scoured her cup, then stacked it with the rest. "Finish your coffee; I would like to show you more of Garobi before you leave. And bring your purse; we will visit the market." Glorya finished her coffee excitedly, then grabbed her purse and headed for the door. Veda had to help her wrap her tigi again, but she found she was starting to get the hang of it. "Strictly speaking it is not necessary to wear while underground, but we find it easier to carry items within it than without it." She showed Glorya a pocket made by one of the folds and winked. Dropping her purse into the pocket, she followed Veda out the door.

It was impossible for her to stay oriented as they traversed tunnel after tunnel. Some supported only unidirectional traffic while others were wide enough for two-way, and still others were large enough to function as roads for carts. Glorya saw no beasts of burden or any other sort; instead, carts were pulled by people, sometimes many at once as they had done on the trip to Garobi. After a dizzying, but short journey, they arrived at the grand hall Mavu had navigated the day before, and Veda took Glorya's arm. "Stay close; it is easy to get lost." The two wound through the jostling crowd, eventually arriving at a narrower end of the hall that sloped upward gently. Stalls full of produce and merchandise lined each wall with plenty of room to pass between, and Glorya felt a fresh breeze brush past her face. This must open to the outside, she noted as she began to peruse the stalls.

Most of the vendors sold practical items—tigi, sandals, food, and the like—but as they made their way down the lane one stall caught Glorya's eye. The light from the nearby lamps glittered off of a multitude of gemstones and polished, precious metals, casting a dazzling display onto the ceiling and walls. The effect was fascinating, and she found herself drifting toward it out of curiosity.

"Ah, you've found the jewelers' stalls," Veda said, taking in the light show herself for a moment before following. "You'll find no better prices than here. They always mark up the items they make and sell at the ports. Some you cannot even find beyond the hills, like this one." She indicated a snaking golden chain on the corner of one of the tables. Rubies dangled from its length at measured intervals, and each end held one half of an intricately worked clasp in the shape of a scorpion. "It is customary for Zhedabans to wear a chain somewhere on their body—the more chains, the wealthier the person. Many times they are gifted by families as a child comes of age. Come, there must be one that will suit you." She cast an experienced eye along the table as Glorya hesitantly joined her.

"They look expensive," she hazarded. When Veda quoted her a price (with the caveat that negotiating was expected, even encouraged), she was startled; most of what she saw was well within what she could afford.

Veda chuckled. "Here in the hills we have more gems than we have food. Many of our craftsmen and women live here, and we have no need to transport things to sell them, so the prices are low." She ran her fingers across another golden chain, this one wider and studded with sapphires. "Do you like blue? Green? Either would look very well with your skin and hair."

Glorya thought for a moment. Jewelry wasn't something she'd ever considered, as it wasn't practical on a farm or aboard a ship, but she could well afford at least a small item, and it would give her something to remember her trip. "Blue is the color of the sky after a storm has passed," she mused aloud.

The two of them spent the next few minutes perusing the jewelers' stalls to find the right chain for Glorya. They landed on a sturdy golden rope with sapphires dangling from the ends that clasped as a lariat. It could be worn as a necklace or around the waist, and Glorya chose to wind it around her waist in the Zhedaban style for the duration of her visit.

After they were finished at the market, Veda took Glorya to meet the caravan master who had offered her passage. He was tall and of large girth, his dark brown tigi embroidered with gold thread around the bottom. His black hair showed no touch of gray despite the smile lines around his eyes and mouth, and he greeted Veda warmly. "Many greetings, Veda! I see you've brought my charge." He switched fluidly to Glorya's language as they approached. She responded with the polite indoor greeting she'd learned the night prior, introducing herself as Lori. "Nice to meet you, Lori. Veda failed to mention your loveliness." He sketched a graceful bow despite his bulk as Glorya colored slightly. "I am Ruja. Would you care to join us for lunch?" Glorya looked to Veda, who agreed perfunctorily. "Come! We will meet the men and women who will be our companions for the next two and a half weeks." He led the way up the ramp and past the last of the vendor stalls, around a broad turn in the walkway, and into the same area they'd used to park their cart when they'd first arrived in Garobi. As they passed, Glorya greeted her crew mates from the Tezhu as they unloaded goods and carried them down the broad tunnel. Many smiled and returned her greeting.

Ruja stopped at a larger cave close to the exit and ushered them in. "Come, come, we are just in time." A group of ten or so men and women were just sitting down at a makeshift table made of stacked cargo crates with a cloth draped over them. Most looked up at their approach, noticed Glorya, stared for a moment, then greeted the newcomers before beginning their meal. Ruja seated Veda and Glorya to his left and right, handing them each a piece of flatbread wrapped around what seemed to be some sort of heavily-seasoned tuber, then started into his own without ceremony. "My mother is an excellent cook," he said around a mouthful of flatbread. Glorya took a bite and found it much to her liking.

They ate and made small talk, and when the meal was finished Glorya was introduced to the group. Few of them understood Glorya's language, so she used her limited Zhedaban to learn names and occupations. Veda deliberately did not mention Glorya's particular talents, instead listing her as a hired deckhand.

After lunch Veda showed Glorya the rest of Garobi. It turned out she had seen the main portion of it, but there existed a warren of tunnels underneath the settlement that connected the living areas with the mines and smithies. Common areas were lit with lamps that burned some form of low-smoke oil, but individual apartments were responsible for their own lighting. Ventilation was built into every portion of the settlement through intricately engineered shafts designed to catch crosswinds off the desert and force the movement of air through the caves. Glorya was fascinated.

Eventually they wound their way back to Mavu's dwelling. Veda stayed for dinner that evening and was able to translate Glorya's thanks to the family for their hospitality before taking her own leave. "I am honored to know you," she said in parting, then gestured her farewell.

Glorya went to bed early in anticipation of a very early start the next day.

Mavu woke her at some indeterminate time that Glorya's body told her was far too early. "You have a visitor from Ruja's caravan. It is time to go. Bring your pack." She rose and ambled back down the hall.

In minutes Glorya had her pack on her shoulder and joined Mavu and their guest in the common room. She recognized the man's face from the prior day—one of Ruja's security detail, though she couldn't recall his name. He stood as she entered the room and greeted her in Zhedaban, and she returned the greeting in kind, taking stock of his appearance. He had removed his tigi out of politeness when he entered, so she could see that he had three chains wound about various portions of his body. Most were simple, but one ended in a charm with an emblem she didn't recognize. His build suggested a life of hard labor or combat, and judging by the scars he bore and the manner of his bearing she suspected the latter.

Mavu took Glorya's hand and gave it a matronly squeeze, wishing her luck. "Come visit anytime," she told Glorya, then helped her put on her tigi. Glorya found she could almost do it herself at this point, but she knew Mavu liked to fuss over her family and guests whenever she could. Donning her pack, she gestured for the guard to lead and took her leave, thanking Mavu again for her help.

The man set off at a brisk pace down the foot traffic tunnels, which were surprisingly busy given the time of day, and led them back to the same cargo cave they'd had lunch in the day prior. Ruja was waiting at the entrance to greet Glorya. "Good morning, Lori! I trust you slept well?" She nodded in response, still slightly embarrassed by the merchant's ingratiating manner and not fully awake yet. "We leave as soon as you are ready."

"Please don't wait any longer on my account," Glorya replied. Ruja nodded, then gestured and spoke to the crew. Two large carts with four people pulling each began to trundle forward out of the cave system. The remaining four crew, Glorya and Ruja included, pulled up their hoods and set out beside the carts into the desert night.

The first week's travel passed uneventfully. Ruja was a wealth of information on everything Zhedaban—culture, geography, social nuance, and, of course, language—and seemed to genuinely enjoy waxing eloquent whenever possible. Glorya continued her linguistic education by learning many of the gestures used for caravan coordination activities, such as stop, go, load, and unload, and a few emergency gestures, like attack and sandstorm. Ruja didn't think it was likely they would meet up with bandits, but about eight days in Glorya noticed his gaze wandering across the horizon with increasing frequency.

She decided to ask about it during their midday break the next day. They had all been taking turns at pulling the carts; Glorya had been doing so out of a need to escape the constant conversation from Ruja, but found that at mealtimes he was inescapably ebullient. He would fuss briefly over her request to help pull, then move on to whatever topic came to mind. She fended off more questions about her homeland by remarking that she was amazed how far she could see in the desert compared to her home, likening it to the sea.

"Indeed, it is much like the ocean," Ruja replied, taking a bite of his lunch and searching the horizon. "It has its doldrums...and its dangerous places."

"How so?" Glorya asked, cocking her head in a very Zhedaban gesture of questioning without thinking.

Ruja noticed it and smiled wanly. "You may have noticed that the desert has changed as we have traveled. It is...difficult to explain to someone not raised among the sands, but there are certain aspects we look for to try to predict the sandstorms. This particular part of our route is safer from bandits than most, but riskier due to the like-lihood of a storm regardless of which time of year you travel. It is also faster and more direct than many."

Glorya chewed her meal thoughtfully. "What do you do if one comes?" she asked.

"Wrap our faces with our tigi, find high ground... and pray." Ruja stood somewhat nervously. "If you will excuse me, I need to speak with Vizhe before we rest." He excused himself politely, then hurried off to speak with the head of the guard.

Exactly how dangerous is this route? Glorya wondered and resolved to check for herself before taking her nap. She finished her lunch, settled herself a short distance away from the rest of the group, and closed her eyes, ostensibly sleeping.

Instead, she threw her senses outward. The desert was a fascinating blend of warmer and cooler air currents in constant motion with little to no humidity to condense as they passed. Complete absence of clouds felt strange to Glorya since she'd spent so long on ships and in wetter climates; here, even the stratosphere felt desiccated. Her range of perception extended further than her physical vision and she was able to gauge the strength of the wind for miles in every direction. I should probably keep a weather eye out from now on, she thought just before she dropped off for a rest.

Starting that afternoon Glorya began her usual at-sea routine of scanning the skies every hour. Ruja wasn't the only one who was nervous; there was a hush over most of the group, as if everyone was fixated elsewhere. The night proved uneventful, but none slept soundly.

In the early hours of the morning, just before sunrise, Glorya took her turn on the cart. She found it easier to hide her weather scanning while holding onto something so she didn't wander as she walked. Closing her eyes briefly, she reached out further and further, finding only the ever-present winds...but there was something different about them. Far to the north the wind had developed a pattern and was pushing in the same direction. It seemed too weak to cause a problem, but as she watched, it found a flatter section among the dunes and came to life. Glorya could feel it churn up the sands, whipping them into a solid wall as it started toward their caravan.

Her eyes snapped open, searching the terrain. High ground, Ruja said. The caravan was already halfway up a ridge that would carry it to the highest point around. That'll have to do. She closed her eyes and tried to gauge the speed of the storm.

A shout startled her as she watched the winds. They've seen it; time to watch for instructions. Glorya looked around at the hand signals flurrying in the predawn light, catching "sandstorm" and an indication of direction: up the ridge. She pulled at the cart along with her team, two more people joining them for greater speed. Glorya found herself next to the guard who had summoned her from Mavu's dwelling—Vizhe, she recalled absently. He barely took notice of her, instead covering his face as much as possible and applying himself to the cart.

They made it to the ridge just as the wind picked up. A wall of sand raced across the desert from the north as far as the eye could see in either direction—further, Glorya knew, as she watched the group stack up behind the carts. They packed in as tightly as possible and wound their tigi around their faces, covering every inch of skin. Glorya followed suit.

The sand thumped into their carts all at once. Sand swirled around her ankles and up the bottom of her tigi, which she drew tighter against her skin. She could feel it beating at the hood around her head and used her other hand to hold it in place. No sound penetrated the wind's wrath for what felt like an eternity, and then Glorya became aware of a creaking sound very close by. Peeking was out of the question...unless she could shield just her eyes...

The creaking sounded again, and Glorya mustered the courage to create a tiny no-wind zone around her eyes. It deadened the gale enough for her to see what was happening within her immediate vicinity. Most of the crew was seated on the lee side of the carts, with a few still standing against them. It was the carts that were creaking; they were broad side to the wind straddling the dune ridge and were loaded high enough that they were starting to tip as the wind gusted. They'll crush everyone. I have to do something. Glorya pushed back the small voice in her mind that reminded her about how Zhedabans felt about sunchasers and their lack of success in conquering the sandstorms and went to work.

Immediately she could see why so many sunchasers failed. The winds were too strong to face head on or try to cancel out directly or en masse—but they could be negated just enough to shelter a caravan if one was skilled enough. Glorya began by expanding the dead zone around her eyes to encompass her head, then her body. Good. That should work. As a test, she tried to simply lessen the wind around her instead of negating it completely, but the storm was too strong; even at half potency it was enough to fling sand into her eyes and sting her skin. No taking chances, then. She began to expand the negation zone outward from herself, surrounding the caravan, just as the lead cart swayed dangerously toward the people it shel-tered. It listed drunkenly, then righted itself and thumped back and forth a few times before settling into the sand once again.

Relieved, Glorya checked the storm to see how long she would need to shield them. The winds were slack-ing off to the north of them, but it would still be a few minutes before things died down. She began picking the winds apart wherever she had the spare energy, but before long simply holding the shield around the caravan was all she could manage. The sand still floated past the carts to accumulate on any exposed surface, but it no longer stung skin.

Finally the winds began to slacken after what seemed like an eternity. In reality, the sun had barely cleared the horizon, but she felt as if she'd been pulling the cart all day with no stops. Opening her eyes, Glorya looked around to see if everyone had made it through the storm.

They were all staring at her. Glorya's face burned as she realized they knew her for what she was. Looks like I might be going the rest of the way on my own. The guard who had pulled the cart next to her was staring down at her as if seeing her for the first time, his rough face unreadable and silent. Then he blinked, reached down, and took her hand in both of his. They were large, callused hands, and Glorya's pale skin disappeared between them as he bowed over her hand in what seemed to be a gesture of deep respect. He straightened, let go, and moved away as another member of the crew stepped forward to do the same.

One by one they filed silently past to make the same gesture. An uncommonly quiet Ruja came last, and Glorya did her best not to recoil as he took her hand and bowed over it. "You are not what you seem, flame-hair," he said as he straightened and let her go. Glorya wiped her hand on the inside of her tigi as if it was cold or dirty. "You have saved my crew and my caravan. You have done what no other like you has done before in the history of my people. How can I repay you?"

"There is no debt," Glorya replied, embarrassed. "I need your help to get back to Joveru so that I might continue to find work. That is all."

"That I can do," Ruja replied.

The caravan traveled a few more hours before stopping midday. Glorya found she didn't have the strength to help pull the cart after her working earlier in the day, instead trudging along beside it. She collapsed in the shade when they stopped and slept deeply until Ruja woke her up to continue their journey. When she nearly fell for the third time out of exhaustion later in the afternoon Vizhe lifted her unceremoniously onto the cart and took a place helping to pull it. Glorya was too tired to fight it and fell asleep to the gentle rocking.

A week later Glorya strolled into Juma's inn, stopping by the door to unwrap her tigi before finding a seat. She

caught the innkeeper's eye as she floated between tables
and greeted her in Zhedaban from across the room. Juma's eyes twinkled as she gestured for Glorya to wait a
moment, then dropped dishes off in the kitchen and joined
Glorya at her table. "It is good to see you again! I see you
have learned much about Zhedaba." She took in the two
golden chains draped around Glorya's waist and her eyebrows rose. "And made a name for yourself!"

Glorya blushed slightly. "I helped a caravaneer on my
way back to Joveru, that's all." She fingered the finer of
the two chains, which tinkled with tiny medallions down
its length as it moved.

"That is Ruja's merchant mark, unless I am wrong,"
Juma said as she squinted at the tiny details. "You must
have done a great thing for him to gift this to you." Glorya
shrugged noncommittally in response. "Keep your secrets,
then, if Zhedaba will let you, but know that few tales of
the desert stay in the desert," Juma warned as she lifted
herself off of the chair she'd settled into. "Will you be
staying long? Can I get you lunch?"

"Lunch would be lovely," Glorya replied with a smile.

OCEAN'S END

Glorya took one last look at the port town of Jogete, then turned to face the docks, her eyes squinting in search of the massive ocean-going ship she was to board. Apprehension knotted her shoulders; she'd spent the better part of a year and a half working the Zhedaban coast, learning the language and customs, and generally making a name for herself, but this voyage promised challenges she couldn't yet fathom. They would spend eight weeks on the water before putting in to the only known port in Temalingar, the western continent.

Working off the coast of Zhedaba felt like a short cruise away from home; in fact, she'd managed a short vacation during the harvest season last year to see her sister and parents and fill them in on her deeds of derring-do. But Temalingar...she knew of no one who had made the journey themselves, only secondhand accounts. Most had only been once—if they lived to tell about it.

Shaking off her fears, Glorya caught sight of the largest three-master she'd ever seen and realized she'd found her destination. She reminded herself that any vessel with her aboard was far more likely to have a successful journey, massive hull notwithstanding. Her ground-eating strides took her right up to the gangplank, where a busy Zhedaban man in sailing clothes stopped her with a signal and barely a glance.

She made the appropriate signs in return, then addressed him in his native tongue, the words falling out of her mouth without thought. "I am Glorya Sunchaser, reporting to the Shima to serve on its cross-ocean voyage." The man's eyes shot upward and took in her copper hair, pale skin, and green eyes, then nodded and gestured her up the gangplank and aboard the vessel.

The cargo hold was open, and Glorya skirted it as cranes lowered crates of food and barrels of water in an endless stream. She hadn't given much thought to the amount of provisions they would need for such a long trip with no way to stop for supplies, and the pile of cargo on the docks waiting to be loaded was staggering. Idly, she wondered what they would be bringing back that was so valuable someone would make such an expensive journey for it.

Movement on the quarterdeck caught her attention, and Glorya realized the bosun's mate had been trying to get her attention for some time. Guiltily she signed her acknowledgment and wove through the organized chaos that signaled imminent departure.

The bosun himself was a man of late middle age, with salt and pepper hair and a trim beard that was further to white. He acknowledged Glorya, took in her attire, and signed to the bosun's mate to continue preparations.

"You come highly recommended," he began without preamble, in Zhedaban. "The people of my country do not often praise those with your talents."

"Their esteem brings me honor—" Glorya paused to gesture respect "—which I will endeavor to maintain aboard this ship."

The bosun nodded. "You speak well. What skills do you possess other than your weatherworking?"

"I can mend ropes, climb rigging, and work the sails with direction, and I have a strong back for whatever else is needed of me." The gesture for looking for work or offering assistance showed ample calluses on her ever-pale palms, and the bosun nodded approvingly.

"Stow your belongings and report to the crow's nest to scout the weather for departure with the tide." Glorya gave the Zhedaban equivalent of a salute and hustled to grab a berth before swarming up the rigging and depositing herself into the crow's nest.

Her new vantage point emphasized the sheer size of the Shima. Its three masts boasted the huge, triangular sails favored by Zhedaban ships. The sheets themselves were uncharacteristically plain, like the rest of the ship, bearing no embroidery or paint to show their wealth or battle prowess. Either this was her maiden voyage or she preferred to appear less than she was, perhaps to avoid the attention of any would-be pirates. The deck's length ran three times its width and sported guns fore and aft that were larger than the cannons she was used to seeing on merchants. Thinking back to her approach down the docks, Glorya recalled seeing gun ports cut into the sides, as well. What kind of vessel is this? she wondered as she cast her thoughts into the skies.

The winds, it seemed, were favorable, and they cast off not long after Glorya gave the all-clear for the weather. Climbing down reluctantly, she busied herself by joining the crew in raising the ship's enormous anchor, watching as it settled into its housing. They secured the windlass and one of the crew threw a smaller chain across the anchor itself to keep it nestled close to the hull. Glorya could see evidence of a recent scraping for barnacles on both the anchor and the hull. Not her first voyage, then. She filed the information away and made herself useful elsewhere as they got underway.

Once the Shima cleared the bay, the crew loosed the sheets and let the ship have her head. Glorya marveled at the sheer yardage of cloth above her as she squinted into the clear sky and listened to the stringent cries of the shore-gulls chasing them out into the open water.

The rigging above her was wholly unfamiliar; pieces of it made sense, but they connected to others in places she didn't expect. Guns, sails, deck compartments that had no obvious purpose, a giant skin-drum on the quarterdeck... the Shima was a fascinating puzzle that Glorya couldn't wait to piece together—

"Sunchaser to the quarterdeck!"

—as soon as she had the chance, of course.

The captain of the Shima stood beside his helmsman, feet apart, hands behind his back. Glorya approached from the starboard side, taking the man's measure as she approached. He was Zhedaban, but wore breeches and a shirt in the northern fashion, like her, though they were far more colorful than her own; oranges and yellows danced across his collar in a fiery procession that rivaled the setting sun. He was broad of shoulder and dark of skin and hair, like many of his countrymen, and wore a mustache that flowed into his thick beard in one grandiose sweep. She put his age somewhere in his forties, though she'd noticed that years on the sea were often worn more heavily on the faces that saw them pass. He regarded his crew with a keen eye, gesturing here and there to his first mate and watching with satisfaction as the men and women on deck wove back and forth in the intricate dance that brought the ship around to its proper course.

He turned as she approached and held out a callused hand in the northern fashion of greeting. "Welcome aboard, Sunchaser," he rumbled in her native tongue as she shook the proffered hand.

Turning the greeting around, she made the gesture for polite respect to a superior and replied in Zhedaban, "I am honored to serve, Captain."

He grinned and clapped her on the shoulder, making her stumble a step closer to the railing. "I can see you're going to do well here," the captain declared as he nodded to the first mate, who took over supervision of the crew. "I am Bedu, captain of the Shima. I assume you have a berth?" Glorya nodded. "And your things are secured? We often see rough seas this time of year." Again Glorya nodded, though mentally she made a note to double check how well she'd stowed her things next chance she got. "Good. Bosun tells me you have sailing experience; was any of it military?"

The question took her aback, but Glorya shook her head. "It was not listed as a requirement in your advert, sir."

"Indeed. We look for crew who have served, but in your capacity it is not necessary, even if it is desirable." The captain pondered for a moment, then continued. "Have you sailed on a vessel the size of the Shima?" he asked.

"No, sir; the largest vessels I have worked with were daba," she replied, using the Zhedaban word for the two-masted merchant vessels that plied the coast. Many were large, but none came close to the size of the Shima.

"Then you have never crossed the ocean?" The captain's eyebrows shot up as Glorya shook her head. He nodded to the first mate, who had kept an ear peeled in case he was needed in their conversation. The shorter, slighter man pulled a whistle from his breast pocket and blew a single, clean note that soared over the growl of the wind and summoned every eye on the deck. Within seconds, all was still.

Captain Bedu spoke into the silence, his voice carrying well despite the wind's attempts to steal his words. "Hear ye, hear ye, Glorya Sunchaser is our ship's talisman this voyage. May she prove a boon greater than any the Shima has yet seen!" A cheer went up from the crew, and those who were not needed to keep the ship moving gathered at the bottom of the stairs Glorya had ascended. Many had made a gesture much like one she knew as warding from evil, but slightly askew.

The captain chuckled. "It is considered lucky to have at least one crew member aboard who has not crossed the sea, as beginner's luck may rub off on the rest of the crew. They expect you on the deck; come see me when you're done and we'll get you started." Nodding a dismissal, he stepped back toward the helm and resumed command of the ship.

Bemusedly, Glorya descended the stairs, unsure of the crowd before her. As she neared they parted down the middle, many reaching out to touch the hem of her shirt or her sleeve, and one by one they leaned close enough to share small pieces of wisdom. Stow your gear as low as you can below your bunk. Make sure the cargo stays close to the keel. Use a safety line in bad weather. Tidbits of knowledge gained through experience floated into Glorya's mind as she passed, and she grasped at them, doggedly committing them to memory and nodding as she did.

After short minutes that seemed much longer, Glorya exited the throng and found herself in the middle of the deck. The group behind her waited expectantly, and she turned, fumbling for something to say in response. "May all your wisdom guide us on our journey," she said, gesturing for respect of elders and betters. The group responded with the same not-quite-warding sign she'd seen earlier and dispersed.

Glorya climbed the stairs to the quarterdeck once again, her mind reeling with the new information she'd gained as she rejoined the captain and first mate. The former nodded in satisfaction as he watched the shoreline recede in the distance and turned, acknowledging Glorya with a gesture. "You wished to see me?" she asked as she gestured awaiting orders.

"I did," Captain Bedu replied. "Each person on my ship has a place, and each one knows it like the back of their hand. Before we journey far together, I must tell you yours." Glorya nodded as the captain paused, then continued. "First, I must know your strengths. You work weather, but where do you measure your skill at it?"

"I have yet to meet a storm I could not best when not opposed by another weatherworker," Glorya replied promptly. "With guidance I can pick and choose which winds may drive the ship and which hinder our journey, and in some cases I can create an area which the weather does not touch." She spoke frankly, without boasting, and the captain nodded.

"But you cannot call the winds," he said, "nor make a storm where there is none."

"Correct, sir," she replied. Captain Bedu pushed himself off the railing beside the helm and gestured for her to follow as he strode aft. "What do you know of naval tactics?" he asked, a shrewd look on his weathered face.

"Very little," Glorya replied, blushing at her ignorance. "I've been trained in ground tactics and hand to hand fighting, but we had no teacher for naval combat, and I've had no reason to learn."

"Then we shall start with the basics," the captain replied. He laid a hand on the large skin-drum attached to the back of the ship. "Do you know what this is?"

"A drum, sir."

"Indeed, but what might be its purpose?"

"I don't know, sir." Glorya shifted from one foot to the other, discomfited.

"It is a warning," Captain Bedu replied. "When this

drum beats, an enemy has been sighted, and the crew must prepare to defend the ship. Each man and woman knows where they are most useful at such a time. Where might you be most useful?" He leveled a measuring stare at Glorya, who broke his gaze to squint across the deck. What could she do if the ship came under attack? She wouldn't be the best choice to help maneuver the ship, at least not until she'd learned more about it, and she didn't know how to work the deck guns. She could help repel boarders, but until then, where could she help the most?

"In the crow's nest?" she finally guessed, picking her favorite spot for its peerless view.

"No," the captain replied. "The first thing the enemy will attack is our mainmast, and if you're in it when we lose it, we lose you. Try again."

Gloyra's brow furrowed. "Certainly not belowdecks..." she ventured.

Captain Bedu shook his head. "No, your place is here, beside whomever is in command of the ship. From here we can coordinate, and you can inform us of any tactical advantage you can provide." Glorya's face cleared as she saw the wisdom in the captain's plan. "Speaking of which, I'll be interested to see what you can do; I'll admit I've worked little with those of your particular talents. Sunchasers are few and far between in Zhedaba, as I'm sure you know." Glorya nodded, her lips a taut line across her face. The captain's visage softened. "Many join the navy, you know," he continued, the brightness in his voice belying his knowledge of how most Zhedaban sunchasers met their ends. Glorya started, meeting the captain's gaze. "Indeed, it is the only place in Zhedaba they can be useful—at least, that is what they're told. Regardless, I have yet to work with one as well trained as yourself, so I shall be interested to see what assistance you can provide."

While they conversed, the ship gracefully dipped out of port and rode the choppy seas of the bay of Jogete, her full belly giving her deck a low profile as she headed toward the bay's mouth. Other vessels joined them on their way out to sea, many of them fishing vessels headed for the rich waters of the coast; they would meet their escorts where the water deepened and follow the shoals of silver fish up and down the coast until they, too, were full. Glorya's eyes followed the groups of smaller vessels as they split off in various directions. Captain Bedu seemed to be searching for something, his eyes finally settling on a particular group of coordinating brightly-colored sails. He gestured to the man at the wheel, pointing out the group as it angled southwest, and the Shima nosed around to follow.

"We have an agreement with the captain of that fishing fleet," he explained, nodding at the boats now ahead of them. "We share their escort until we reach the shipping lanes going and coming, and in return she gets a percentage of our profit from the run. It gives us a day or so of protection before we're on our own." He adjusted his sleeves and turned to survey the horizon.

"Protection from what, sir?" Glorya asked warily.

The captain chuckled. "Pirates, of course," he replied. "Either after our supplies on the way out, or our profits on the way back. We should be safe enough leaving; they know the Shima, and we've been successful enough times that they'll wait for us to return before they strike." Satisfied, he returned his attention to Glorya. "Speaking of which, you said you were trained in hand to hand combat, yes?" She nodded, her head spinning from the conversation's rapid directional changes. "Good. Hit me."

"Sir?" she asked as her brows shot upward.

"Hit me, Sunchaser. If you can. I'd like to see how capable you are." He stood, perfectly relaxed, and regarded her with an amused smile.

Think, Glorya. He's Zhedaban; how do they fight? Glorya shifted her weight into a balanced stance and brought up her guard as she'd been trained to do. Fights with her siblings, then her classmates, then the Zhedaban crews she'd worked with flashed through her mind as she searched for a successful approach. Warily, she feinted with her left hand and watched as Captain Bedu shifted slightly, his longer right arm shooting out with surprising speed to catch her in a counterattack. But she was no longer where he expected her to be, and she watched his eyes grow wider as her right fist slipped inside his reach. He flowed backward just far enough for her uppercut to displace his beard instead of his jaw and smiled broadly, disengaging.

"I'm impressed," he said as he rearranged his beard back into the neatly-brushed shape it had previously held. "Where did you say you were trained?"

"Weatherwatch, sir, and at home besides." Glorya stood little straighter and added, "I have brothers."

Captain Bedu chuckled. "So you do. You'll train with the second rank, then, at dawn. I'll want you in the crow's nest every four hours for a weather check, with the exception of midnight so you can get some rest. For now, see the bosun for an assignment. Unless you have any more question or concerns, that is…" He lifted an eyebrow.

"No, sir," she replied, gesturing respect for authority.

"Then I will see you at dinner. You are dismissed." The captain turned toward the first mate, leaving Glorya to cast about the deck for the bosun.

He was a small man, wiry and strong, with a clean-shaven face and white hair. The work on deck seemed to flow around him, carrying him to his next task in the same way the currents carried the ship through the pass and out into the open water. Glorya hailed the man and found herself drawn into the crew's inexorable rhythm.

The first day of their voyage passed in a blur of new information and experiences. For one, the Shima's crow's nest was taller than any Glorya had climbed, and despite her comfort with heights and ropes she found her hands sweating as she climbed the final third of the way to her perch for the noon watch. Safely ensconced on the small bordered platform, Glorya took a moment to inhale the salty air and survey her surroundings. The view at this height was unparalleled, and she was able to see the entire fishing fleet and most of its escort in good detail. If she squinted, she could almost make out another set of sails behind them…

"Captain! Sails on the horizon!" The call went up from below her, somewhere around the stern.

Captain Bedu said something to the helmsman and the Shima began angling out to sea. "We'll leave them behind; they won't follow far," he boomed across the deck, and a cheer went up from the crew. "Full speed ahead!" A complex dance began below Glorya, who watched raptly as various sails were loosed, others furled, and the huge ship danced away from its escort. Remembering her own responsibilities, she took stock of the sails in use and cast her thoughts to the winds, picking through them to reduce any directional ambiguities she could find, and was pleased to feel them pick up yet more speed. The sails in pursuit vanished from view.

Glorya returned to the deck, exhilarated by the short chase and even more fascinated with the ship and its crew.

In the days that followed, Glorya found herself with little free time. Between her regular weather checks and learning the ropes, her hands and mind were completely occupied from sunup to sundown. At dawn each day she trained in hand-to-hand combat, learning the Zhedaban fighting style and teaching its weaknesses to her comrades in arms. She quickly became proficient with the short blades they favored for shipboard fighting and found herself looking forward to the exercise each day.

The weather at sea felt different from any Glorya had sensed; it was both wild and free, but also driven by larger forces beyond her ability to detect. With so little to stop it the wind felt similar to the desert, but the humidity and cloud cover, along with the ocean currents and their temperature vagaries, stirred the weather into a giant, complex system that was impossible to predict. Glorya could see why the captain had her check the weather every four hours at minimum, and occasionally would ask for updates every two. Thankfully, the worst they ran across was a bad rainstorm or three, which Glorya was able to help them manage without disrupting the weather for the entire continent on which Zhedaba sat—at least, as best as she could tell.

Despite the amount of work it took to crew such a large ship, there were the occasional lulls in the journey. When they crossed the midway point the crew took a half day's rest, many producing small leisure items such as musical instruments or books or some of the intricate fishbone models the sailors liked to craft. Glorya learned how to dance in the Zhedaban style, and the captain himself even condescended to join in the festivities, whirling and twisting a colorful path through the other dancers around the deck. Strong drink was passed around, and the crew celebrated until well after the sun had dipped below the horizon.

The Shima itself became less of a mystery as Glorya shadowed the various crew members, learning the ins and outs of the vast ship. One by one the extra pieces of rigging, sails, boxes, and compartments revealed their purpose, and by the time they sighted the coast of Temalingar after a full eight weeks at sea, she could fill in for at least half the deckhands. Captain Bedu would occasionally stroll past and nod or give a gentle correction as she performed various duties, surprising her with the depth of his knowledge in each task. He was in the midst of an animated explanation of the ship's combat maneuvering when the cry went up that land had been sighted, and the crew's cheers drowned out the rest of his explanation. He smiled good-naturedly and nodded to Glorya, resuming his position on the quarterdeck.

After two months of sailing, every soul aboard the Shima was abuzz with excitement at the prospect of dry land. All energy and effort went toward making into port as fast as humanly possible, and the dock—such as it was—loomed up out of the last rays of the sun at the beginning of the ninth week of their journey. The ship slowed considerably after entering the broad bay containing a single pier that jutted unsteadily into the surf. As they neared, Glorya could see that many of the planks on the dock had holes and others were missing entirely. No cranes protruded from the dockside to assist with unloading, and there was very little bustle around the dock itself; in fact, she counted only three figures on the short, sandy beach before them, one of whom went running toward a set of wooden buildings barely visible beneath the tree cover that loomed at the edge of the coast. The trees themselves were thick-boled and squat, with large, waxy leaves and stout branches, and they sheltered all manner of dense underbrush and scrub plants despite the sandy soil.

There was no time to take in more of the coastline before preparations to dock took precedence. The Shima looked huge next to the dilapidated pier structure, and Glorya was afraid that if they came in too quickly they might knock it down. But the seas were calm and the crew efficient, and the ship bellied up to the dock just close enough to get ropes onto the sparse bollards before dropping anchor. With no welcoming party two of the crew had to jump from the deck to secure the ship before the gangplank could be run out.

Captain Bedu surveyed his ship with one keen eye turned toward the nearby town. Before long a small group detached itself from the unrelenting greenery before them, heading toward the dock. The captain nodded and motioned for the first mate—Zem, Glorya recalled his name—to follow him before debarking the vessel to wait for the local entourage.

Glorya made herself useful any way she could, glancing up periodically to snatch her first glimpses of the Temalingari. From the gently swaying deck she couldn't see much, but as they neared she could tell they were shorter of stature than many of the crew, equally dark-skinned, and had fine, dark hair, but there was something odd about their feet she couldn't quite make out—it was as if they wore strangely-shaped shoes, though there were no visible ties or buckles to hold them on. Their features were finer-boned than she was accustomed to, and even the largest among them was not broad compared with the Zhedaban crew. Captain Bedu towered over the group as a whole. As they approached, the first mate stepped forward, speaking in a low enough voice Glorya couldn't hear them over the sighing of the wind. The oldest-looking member of the delegation stepped forward and made a rough bow, answering in kind without much else in the way of gestures. It was then Glorya realized they were speaking her native tongue as a snippet of conversation floated to her on the wind. She edged closer to the railing, straining to hear more.

"...room in town," the delegate was saying. "Your crew may have to sleep on your boat."

"That is fine," Zem replied, gesturing in Zhedaban by way of translation as he repeated what the other man had said. "We prefer to stay close, especially in poor weather."

"Our portents advise the monsoons will be upon us early this year," the Temalingari delegate advised. "Your return journey may be delayed."

"That is a risk we take each trip." Zem looked to Captain Bedu, who nodded. "May the crew make trips to town for food and drink?" From there, the conversation devolved into the setting of rules for the crew when visiting town, what hours the town kept, and which areas to avoid or frequent. The surrounding swamplands were declared free range, but ill-advised due to predatory animals and other natural hazards. The town itself was called Ma-Reku and sat at the mouth of a large river to take advantage of the rich alluvial delta, though Glorya was at a loss as to how an area prone to severe flooding and covered in dense forestation could be used for farming.

Before long the rules had been set and the crew welcomed, and the delegation returned to Ma-Reku with Captain Bedu in tow. Zem stepped back across the gangplank to give instructions to the bosun, then followed, presumably as support for the captain. Word was passed around the crew that they were granted shore leave to camp or picnic on the beach, but that they would have to wait until the next day to visit the town, as the hour grew late and the villagers would soon be abed. A cheer went up as the crew finished settling the ship for its time in port and began filing down the gangplank to feel the solid ground beneath their feet.

They camped on the beach that night, eager to sleep somewhere that didn't rock constantly. The weather was temperate and mild, and the breeze coming off the ocean prevented disturbance from the insects that plagued anyone who ventured inland. Spare sails were rigged around water barrels and boxes to make impromptu tents, fires were built, food was cooked, and of course merriment followed. Glorya spent most of the evening attempting to satiate her avid curiosity about Temalingar, but it seemed none of the crew knew much about the place despite having visited it before. She gave up when the dancing started and joined in, though something tickled at the back of her mind as she twirled around the fire with the crew. It felt a little like a warning, but she chose to ignore it until the morrow.

That night, the rains came.

By the time Captain Bedu returned to the ship the next morning the waterlogged camp had been struck and the crew had resumed their quarters within the ship. Rain fell in sheets, limiting visibility to no more than a person's height in any direction, and the wind had picked up. Despite the inclement weather the crew was informed they would be unloading for a midmorning trade with the locals, which was met with groans all around. It would take all hands to shift the cargo onto the dock. Once again Glorya wondered what could possibly be valuable enough to make such a long, expensive trip as she watched the crates and barrels pass over the deck and onto the waiting wagons on the dockside. They seemed heavy; the wagons never looked full as they were drawn away by stout men and women, but the effort it took to shift them belied the density of the cargo.

Glorya lent her strong back to the throng on deck, lifting, carrying, even shoving crates and barrels across the deck and over to the hastily-built cranes listing across the docks in the gale. No words were spoken by the loaders or the crew; the first because they couldn't be heard and the latter because a Zhedaban crew needed no speech to communicate. Hand signals cut through the deafening roar of wind and rain and were passed along the chain to their destinations, then back again. Carts were laden and trundled off into town until at last there were no more trade goods to unload. Backs creaked and straightened as the crew trudged back to their quarters to drip dry and await orders.

A few soggy, miserable hours later the captain returned to the Shima, looking as much like a drowned rat as the rest of his crew. "Good news!" he boomed across the too-full room. "We are to be the guests of the Temalingari until such time as the monsoon deity sees fit to let us sail for home." The Zhedaban equivalent of a ruckus ensued at the news, manifesting mostly as the slap of wet clothing as gestures of surprise and disappointment flew across the cabin. Holding up a hand for peace, Captain Bedu continued. "Disappointing as this may seem, I for one will relish this chance to learn more about our trading partners so that we can better serve them in the future. I expect the rest of you to do the same. Conduct yourselves in a manner befitting the honorable crew you are and you will be rewarded with freedom to move about the town and surrounding areas; break the rules and you'll be stuck on this tub for the remainder of the storms." His sharp eye swept across the room, catching every single person before he continued. "I think you will find our hosts generous and kind, if somewhat...different. Remember: their customs are not ours, and we are strange visitors in a strange land. I have yet to learn much about it myself, but as I learn I will pass my knowledge on to you. I would ask that you all do the same." Nods met this latest request, along with a shuffling of feet. "Now, we will keep a minimal watch here aboard the ship, rotating in shifts..." The rest of the captain's address floated across Glorya's consciousness just long enough for her to register that she had not been assigned a watch shift before merging once again with her constant background awareness of the storm above them.

She couldn't find the edge. For the first time in her life, she'd found a storm larger than her senses could comprehend, and it was both terrifying and utterly fascinating all at once. The patterns it wove were intricate and unfamiliar, but she knew that if she could just study them for a while, she would unravel their mysteries...

"Sunchaser." Blinking, Glorya returned her consciousness to the rocking of the ship and pounding of the rain. Zem, the first mate, was standing before her as if waiting for something.

Belatedly, she remembered to show respect. "How may I be of service?" she asked, shaking her head to clear it.

"The locals have one who shares a language with you,"

Zem replied. "The captain wishes your assistance as an interpreter."

"I am at the captain's command," Glorya replied, gesturing for Zem to lead on.

They approached the town through the thundering squall of the monsoon, drenched from head to toe within seconds of opening the door. Visibility was an arm's length ahead, no more. Glorya could see why they wouldn't be leaving port until the storms subsided; to leave in this weather would be suicide.

Before long the sand beneath their feet gave way to stubbly grass, then barely-perceptible bushes on either side of them. Long shadows that might be trees loomed just out of sight, more a presence than a part of the visible landscape. Wind funneled down the path they trod, tugging at their sodden clothing and hair as if to pull them back towards the ship. Glorya made a frustrated sound, remembering who she was, and made a small bubble around them, deflecting the wind and causing the rain to soften as it hit, no longer lashed about by the gale. Zem and Glorya straightened as they entered the town.

Their first sign of civilization was the gentle, insistent tinkling of glass from multiple directions as their feet crossed the threshold between sand and wooden planking. It cut through the sighing of the wind, leading them toward the wooden structures that loomed out of the murky stew of precipitation. Zem seemed to have a particular destination in mind, so Glorya let him lead them past many raised walkways to a central structure that stood a bit higher than the rest. She could barely make out the roof line as they passed under the cover of the broad-leafed trees above. The trees stilled most of the downpour and allowed Glorya to wipe the worst of the moisture from her eyes as they approached a large porch set with benches and chairs. A large opening directly before them was covered with a flap of oiled leather, and from behind it they heard muffled voices. One belonged to Captain Bedu, who spoke in a lightly accented version of Glorya's native tongue.

"I have thirty-four strong crew who can help," he was saying as they parted the curtain and entered the room. The captain sat at a short table across from a very import-ant-looking man in a tall headdress made of brightly-col-ored feathers. Another, shorter man sat to the left of the captain and appeared to be translating his statements for the other man's benefit. Is he the chieftain of the town? Glorya wondered if he was the same man she'd seen on the docks after their arrival.

Captain Bedu looked up as the leather curtain fell closed with a soft susurration. "Ah, my translator has ar-rived," he said, beckoning Glorya closer to the table. She barely had time to survey the room before taking a seat to the captain's right. It was a small, private space with just enough room for the captain, Zem, the town chieftain, his translator, and two guards behind them. The townspeople were of shorter stature than the Zhedaban crew and very fine-boned, with narrow shoulders and long, dexterous fingers. Their faces tended toward hollow cheeks and oval shapes, with almond-shaped brown eyes set large above high cheekbones. Black hair ringed their faces, braided out of the way in intricate patterns.

"We are discussing the terms of keeping our crew in town while the rains fall," Captain Bedu said, shaking Glorya out of her assessment.

"I see," she replied, her native tongue feeling odd, yet comfortable. She had spoken it only sparingly for two years. "How may I help?"

Before anyone could respond a gust of wind blew open the door and a figure ducked through. It was masculine, taller than the rest of the Temalingari present, and almost as broad as the captain. The newcomer shook moisture from the oiled skin he wore over his shoulders, then lowered the hood as he knelt before the group.

The chieftain spoke briefly in a strange language full of trills, odd tones, and vowels that reminded Glorya of a small brook rilling over moss-covered stones. Apparently satisfied, the newcomer stood as their translator said, "This is Rizku, leader of the Monsoon Riders. He is honored among our people." Hearing his name, the man's face turned sharply toward their guests, his piercing glance taking in first the captain, then Zem, before settling on Glorya. His eyes widened almost imperceptibly as he took in her sodden red hair, then resumed their narrowed scan of the room. As he turned she caught sight of a long, jagged scar running the length of his jaw. Like his compatriots he wore his jet-black hair intricately braided, but also tied back in a practical fashion to keep it out of his face. His long hands were scarred, but looked strong. Glorya guessed him to be in his mid to late twenties–barely her elder.

Rizku folded himself onto the floor with his back against the rear wall as soon as he was finished studying the group. His eyes were hooded as conversation picked back up. "As I was saying," Captain Bedu continued, "we were discussing the terms under which the crew could stay in town. I have offered their strong backs and hands to help with planting, building repair, or any other labor they could use, but I know little of Temalingari ways of life. I was hoping Chief Llek could advise us."

He gestured at the man in the headdress, who looked to his translator as Glorya relayed the message to him. After some rapid-fire Temalingari the chief nodded, answering in more gutteral tones.

"Chief Llek will consider this offer and consult his people to see what sort of help they need," the translator replied. "Are there any other services or skilled labor you can offer?"

Glorya cleared her throat. "If I may, Captain," she began, "I am familiar with the farming techniques of my homeland and can lend both hands there." Her gaze became questioning as she ventured her next offer. "I will also offer my services with weatherworking, with my captain's permission." The translator looked puzzled at the new word, so she searched for another. "I am a Sunchaser. I make wind and storms dissipate–make them go away." She gesticulated vaguely, but the man still looked confused. He spoke a string of liquid syllables to the chief, who sat forward a bit in his seat. In the background Rizku narrowed his eyes, whether in interest or suspicion, Glorya couldn't be sure.

"One moment," she said, rising from the table, remembering to gesture to Captain Bedu and bow to Chief Llek before approaching the wind-blown door flap. With a thought Glorya silenced the gale whistling through the flap. Chief Llek sucked air through his teeth, his translator sat up straighter in his chair, and Rizku stood in one fluid motion. All of them fixed their eyes on Glorya, who pointed to herself. "Sunchaser," she said, and dropped the bubble around the doorway, which resumed its flapping immediately. Glorya resumed her seat beside the captain, who nodded uncertainly.

Rizku bent down to speak in Chief Llek's ear. His

words were unintelligible, but his voice carried naturally, a rough bass that cut across the room with ease. The chief nodded, then turned to Captain Bedu. He spoke through his interpreter. "We have need of her skills. Our town has one like her and another that can call wind. They need training. Nargi is not able to do what she can do." He nodded in Glorya's direction.

She looked to Captain Bedu. "With your leave, sir, I'm glad to help," she replied.

"What are her services worth to your people?" Captain Bedu asked through her, a shrewd look in his eye.

The chief conferred briefly with his interpreter and Rizku, then answered, "Her services for the season will pay for one third of your people's supplies for the wet season."

Captain Bedu leaned back in his chair. "That would leave us two thirds to cover with unskilled labor. Besides, you said yourself you have no one who can perform this task. That should be worth at least two thirds of our supplies, maybe more."

"Our town cannot grow enough food for that without a lot of help," Chief Llek replied. "Half is the best I can offer."

"Half and a ten percent discount on what we need to purchase and you have a deal," Captain Bedu answered, settling in his seat. The chief and his interpreter did some brief calculations, then nodded.

"We agree to these terms," the chief said, standing and extending a hand to shake. "This is your tradition for showing agreement, yes?"

Captain Bedu shook the man's hand firmly. "It is, and I look forward to earning our keep." Both men sat across from each other and the atmosphere in the room relaxed.

"There is one more thing I would like to understand," he continued. "Your ways are very different from ours, and we do not wish to insult your hospitality. Can your man give us a list of social rules and laws we must follow?"

"Of course," the interpreter replied as he translated for his chief. "But I cannot write this language, only speak it."

"Allow me to transcribe," Glorya offered. The man nodded, and Chief Llek stood.

"You must have much to do," he said, and Captain Bedu followed suit. "I will speak with my people to see what help they need. My man will tell you what we find." Nodding, the chief vacated the tent through another door flap at the back, leaving Glorya and Captain Bedu with the interpreter and the hulking enigma that was Rizku. The latter had stood as Chief Llek left and continued to stand, not threatening, but obviously interested. Glorya spared him a quick glance before turning her attention to the interpreter and found Rizku studying her intently. She met his gaze, then turned unconcernedly to ask for something to write on. *I bet most folk find him intimidating.* She silently wished him luck; larger and more dangerous men had tried her mettle.

The interpreter produced a piece of some kind of parchment and a grease pencil, handing them to Glorya. She realized absently as she began to copy that the sheet was likely waterproof—vellum, perhaps—and the grease pencil wouldn't run. *Necessity is the mother of invention,* she thought as she began to write. It took the better part of half an hour to write down a complete list of the village's expectations, but by the time they'd finished Glorya was satisfied they understood each other. She took an extra sheet or two of vellum and a pencil and headed back to the Shima with Zem to begin her translation. The trip back confirmed her suspicion; none of the scrawled words ran down the page, and in fact the paper made a wonderful visor to keep out the rain.

As they crossed the edge of the town once again, Glorya looked back briefly to get her bearings; she was due back bright and early the next morning to meet her pupils. The rain had slowed to a steady soaking drumbeat, and she could see almost to the wraparound porch on the hut they had visited. Rizku stood at the bottom of the steps, watching them disappear.

By the time Glorya left the Shima the next day Captain Bedu had two copies of the rules and regulations for staying in port, one in Glorya's native tongue and the other in Zhedaban. He had helped with the translation himself since her command of the written language was not as solid as her speech. Two pages of flowing, beautiful script later Glorya was amazed once again at the man's many talents. He had sent her off with the admonishment that she should eat something before she left, as teaching is often hungry work. It was the same thing her father used to tell her before sending her out into the fields, though she didn't tell the captain that; instead she stopped by the galley and picked up some dried fish wrapped in seaweed and filled her water skin from the overflowing cistern. They would have no shortage of clean water for the journey back.

Glorya set out down the dock on her own just after sunrise, unafraid to make the short journey into town unaccompanied. She'd proven herself handy with and without a weapon and was almost as strong as most of the men on the crew. Still, she kept her eyes open as she passed under the trees, recalling the villagers' recommendations to stay on the path to avoid the creatures that lurked in the forest…

"Sunchaser." Glorya jumped as she spun around to find the interpreter from the previous day's negotiations waiting for her at the edge of town. "Is that the correct way to address you? I apologize if it is not; I have no other name for you, and here we are known by our profession as well as our family and self-name. I am Bunsir." The smaller man bowed politely, one hand over his heart.

"Glorya," she replied, bowing in return, "and 'Sunchaser' is quite appropriate; in fact, I will ask my pupils to refer to me as such, as it is considered an honorific among my people." At the man's quizzical look, she explained, "An honorific is like a profession name; it is respectful to acknowledge someone's competence in what they do." Bunsir made an "ah" sound as the clouds cleared from his expression. "Speaking of my students, where might I meet them?"

"They await you at the edge of the village," Bunsir replied, gesturing toward the path to their left.

Glorya turned and started down the scrub-lined walkway, shortening her stride unconsciously to accommodate the shorter man. "You have a thorough knowledge of my language," she said as they walked. "I'm impressed. You must teach me some of yours so that I may better teach your people—and so that I don't embarrass myself." She smiled to help put the man as ease.

Bunsir smiled in return, his weathered features warming. Glorya realized he was older than she'd thought, perhaps fifty, but still had no gray in his braided hair. Unlike most of the townspeople he wore his half loose, with the top half pulled tight behind his head. Glorya wondered idly if his choice of hairstyle affected the number of wrinkles visible on his face.

"We do not use as many hand movements as your captain does," Bunsir began as they walked. "Our language is much more simple. We bow to show respect, and the rest is mostly words. I can teach you a few on the way." Nodding her assent, Glorya bent all her attention to learning the few greeting words she had time to absorb before meeting her new students. The language was fluid, with rolled r's and flat-sounding l's and vowels in places she didn't expect, but by the time they arrived at the edge of town she could mimic Bunsir's lesson well enough to earn a grin from the man.

The path they trod opened onto a section of beach divided from the docks by a large outlet, which they'd crossed over on a long raised walkway. Sitting on the beach facing them were two nearly identical faces, both long and thin, but one almost imperceptibly more round than the other. Each wore their hair differently; one had his braids tied fastidiously behind his head while the other let the wind whip his freely across his face. Both turned as Glorya and Bunsir approached.

Glorya bowed and repeated the greeting she'd just learned, introducing herself. Her new students grinned and returned the gesture, naming themselves Nargi and Bargi. Nargi was the slimmer-faced one with the stern gaze, which helped Glorya distinguish him from his twin brother, who wore a happy-go-lucky grin. Bunsir looked to Glorya, who surveyed her class with a critical eye in an attempt to emulate her own erstwhile instructors.

Bunsir had brought with them a small awning of sorts to pitch on the sand and cover them while they worked. Glorya helped set it up, calming the winds so that they could set up the sticks that held the oiled cloth aloft without dropping them. Nargi's eyebrows rose as she did so, and Bargi elbowed his brother in the ribs, grinning and speaking rapidly. Finally, when they had a dry work space, Glorya beckoned the twins to sit under the shelter.

"I have been tasked with teaching you how to work the winds—and how to calm them," she began as Bunsir translated. "We will begin as I was taught, by first perceiving, then altering what we can. But before we do so, we must understand that everything we do—every change we make—has consequences." Here she paused for Bunsir to catch up. When her students' faces turned more serious, she continued. "Each storm we disperse might have watered hundreds of fields full of crops. Each wind we call might start a sandstorm across the ocean. And each storm we kindle might grow until it sinks ships and takes lives." Here she paused for effect, watching her pupils register the gravity of her words. They seem to understand this more deeply than I did at first. "In that light, we will learn to control and influence what we must to save lives and livelihoods while leaving the natural cycles of the world intact. Which of you is the sunchaser?" At this last term Bunsir stumbled, unable to translate directly, and instead used gestures and a lengthy description to explain until Nargi raised a tentative hand. "You are able to negate—turn off—the winds your brother calls?" He nodded after the translation finished. "I will teach you what I know of control and help you learn how far your abilities can take you. You—" she turned to Bargi—"are a windwaker?" Again Bunsir stumbled at the translation, and Glorya added, "You make wind?" At the man's barely-contained mirth Glorya realized her comment sounded like a childish joke. She passed a hand across her face and added, "Not that kind of wind." Bargi burst out laughing, answering in a stream of syllables that Bunsir translated only in part due to impropriety.

Glorya spent the entire morning working with her new students. Through the medium of Bunsir she was able to determine that both twins had strong affinities for their talents and that they worked well together—when they chose to. Bargi was by far the more jovial of the two, and Nargi seemed to adamantly oppose his brother's lack of gravitas with an overabundance of his own. But if they could set aside their personalities long enough to coordinate their abilities they would make a fearsome pair.

They broke for lunch when both students showed signs of exhaustion. Glorya guessed it to be late morning, but given the weather it was difficult to tell. She decided to turn the tables and have her students teach her some of their language. Glorya requested Bunsir to stop translating and asked the three of them to treat her as they would a child first learning to speak. Bargi lit up at the idea, and Nargi looked grudgingly admiring as she repeated the words they used, pointing at objects as they walked back to town for lunch. They stopped at a hut near the center of town whose open windows fanned out tantalizing, exotic smells. The structure itself was simple, with the same wraparound porch as the rest of the buildings Glorya had seen and a skin covering for a door. As they approached a figure stooped through the frame, stopping as if to bar their way.

Glorya bowed and introduced herself in Temalingari, recognizing Rizku from his silhouette. He stood a head taller than she, forcing her to look up as she approached to meet his eyes. An interminable half minute drew out as he studied her minutely, his hawk-like gaze boring into her as he sought to take her measure. Just as she began to wonder if she'd erred somehow, the taller man bowed, then moved aside to let them enter, watching each member of the group as they passed inside the building. Bargi received the most scrutiny and a near scowl before the door fell closed behind them.

"Well said, Sunchaser," Bunsir said with obvious relief. "You have begun to gain his respect. Please, have some lunch." He gestured toward the tables of food laid out before them, which the twins had already begun to pillage. Nargi chose from a plate of sweet-smelling fruit while Bargi heaped his own plate with roast meat. It looked and smelled like pork, but Glorya couldn't be sure. She decided to play it safe and chose a whole roasted fish and fresh-baked bread for her own fare. The twins spent their lunch break teaching her words for the things they ate and pointing out other useful items around the hut while Bunsir attempted to bridge the language gap and fill in any blanks the brothers left. By the time they'd finished Glorya felt more confident in the few words she'd retained and resolved to practice them with the crew that evening.

They returned to the beach through a howling gale only to find their awning half pulled out of the sand by the blistering wind. Again Glorya calmed the winds long enough to erect the structure, but this time she felt a tentative thread of assistance from Nargi. Smiling encouragingly, she nodded for him to take over as they finished weighing down the rogue side of the awning. For a moment all stayed calm, but before long the wind kicked back in with a vengeance as if angry that it had been deprived of its sport. Nargi's face darkened with frustration, but Glorya placed a hand on his arm to encourage him, earning an audible gasp from Bunsir and a sharp, questioning look from Nargi.

She withdrew her hand as if burned. "What did I do wrong?" Glorya asked warily. "I apologize if I gave offense; your customs are still new to me."

Nargi shook his head and spoke briefly. "You did not offend because you are new to our ways," Bunsir explained. "But you should know that men and women do not touch outside of a shared home in our culture." Glorya's mouth made an O as she nodded, making mental notes.

"I do not believe that was covered in our rules yesterday," she replied. "I will be sure to tell the rest of the crew. How do you make apologies?" she asked Bunsir, who showed her a deeper bow and a new word. Glorya repeated this to Nargi, who returned her bow, but slightly less deeply. So the bow itself has nuance. She resolved to write notes as soon as she returned to the Shima and debrief the captain on her findings.

The rest of the afternoon was spent instructing the twins in the basics of weatherworking. It was slow work due to the language barrier, and by the time they broke for dinner Glorya was exhausted. She'd underestimated how much work it was to teach. Bunsir invited her to dine with the rest of the group, but Glorya declined, desiring to get back to the ship and write what she'd learned before she fell asleep where she stood. She bade them farewell and turned toward the path to the docks just as she felt eyes watching her retreat. Turning for a moment she spotted a tall shape mostly obscured by the rain. She drew herself up to her full height and pinned the figure with her own stare, then bowed just enough to be seen through the drizzle. As she turned to go, the figure bent in return, copying her gesture with meticulous exactness before turning on its heel and stalking out of sight.

Glorya let the wind whip her hair about as she trudged back to the Shima, entirely too exhausted to do anything but put one foot in front of the other. At one point she thought she caught a flicker of movement in the trees to her right, but by the time she'd snapped her head around to face it there was nothing there. Jumping at shadows, she thought as she continued on toward the ship that was her home away from home.

Captain Bedu was waiting for her belowdecks. "Ah, Sunchaser," he said as Glorya closed the hatch behind her and shook off the worst of the water from her clothing. "How was your first day with pupils?" He addressed her in her own language, and she replied in Zhedaban, thoroughly tired of language learning for the day and ready for something more recently familiar.

"It went well, sir," she replied as she pulled off her boots, dumping water from them before setting them next to her bunk. "I have begun to learn their language, and they have begun to learn what's needed for them to work the weather with more skill. Both have learned bad habits that must be corrected, but they are fast learners and I think will do well." Here she took a dry towel offered to her by Zem, gesturing for deep gratitude before continuing. "I have also learned that their culture does not allow men and women to touch unless they share a home, which would have been good to mention yesterday while they were outlining rules."

The captain's brow furrowed slightly. "That does seem like important information," he replied in Zhedaban, gesturing concern and curiosity. "I wonder if they withheld it knowingly or considered it something so obvious they thought it common across cultures. I suppose it matters not; I will pass the word to the crew." Captain Bedu studied Glorya for a moment, taking in the dark circles under her eyes and unusual paleness in her complexion. "You look exhausted. Why don't you get something to eat, then get some rest," he suggested gently. "We can speak more tomorrow." Glorya nodded, gestured thanks, and trundled off to find some dinner before changing into dry clothes and falling into bed.

The next week was a blur of teaching, learning, eating, writing, and sleeping, most of it done while soaking wet. The Temalingari never seemed to mind the constant damp; "better than the dry season, where everything is dust," they would say when she asked. Bargi and Nargi proved to be promising students, correcting their faults almost as quickly as Glorya could point them out. Individually they were precocious to a fault, but together they were unstoppable. Glorya was beginning to wonder what they could achieve if they truly learned to work together. The twins were connected on a very deep level despite their obvious differences.

On their eighth day of instruction they found Rizku waiting at their makeshift beachfront schoolroom. Bunsir bowed respectfully and asked a question Glorya could barely make out over the wind, which she dampened for their conversational benefit. Nodding his thanks, Bunsir repeated his question. Rizku rattled off a matter-of-fact reply, then nodded at both of the tent's occupants and strode purposefully back toward the village.

Bunsir turned to Glorya, his face closed. "Rizku says they are leaving today," he began without meeting Glorya's eyes. "The flood waters have risen to the point where more delay could cost lives. Nargi and Bargi are needed upstream to help keep our settlements from being swept away."

"Is that what the Monsoon Riders do?" Glorya asked as she struck the tent, unwilling to leave it exposed on the beach when not in use.

"They ride the river, giving aid to the villages that do not weather the storms well," Bunsir explained as he helped package the cloth and ropes into bags for later use. "Their rafts carry both food and supplies for repairs to the outer areas so the people do not starve or die of exposure."

"A noble calling," Glorya mused.

"The noblest," Bunsir agreed. "Which is why they are given special dispensation to break with our customs— they give their freedom and often their lives so that others may live." They trudged up the beach toward the village, wind and rain lashing about the edges of the bubble Glorya formed around them. "Rizku is the oldest, at twenty-nine, and many are amazed he has lived this long."

So I was right about his age, Glorya thought triumphantly. "Is the river so dangerous?" she asked aloud, realizing that in his twenty-nine years Rizku had likely seen more peril than half her crew.

"There is a reason we worship the river god," Bunsir replied patiently. "He is very unpredictable, and as he gives us fertile land for planting, he also takes from us many of our people before their time." At this his expression grew heavy, and Glorya could almost see him listing out the loved ones he'd lost to the weather's deadliness. Her heart ached for him as she thought of what it must be like to work so hard and still lose those closest to you. Her brothers' faces flashed unbidden in her mind and she scrubbed at one eye, hoping they were safe and warm at their homestead.

They were silent for the rest of their journey back to the village, where they stopped at the chief's building in the middle of town. Captain Bedu appeared around the same time, and the three of them entered the large structure together. They were met by the chief, who was seated in his usual chair, and his two guards. Rizku also stood behind his chief and just to his left, surveying the group with an inscrutable expression.

Glorya bowed as low as Bunsir and greeted the chief in similar fashion. Captain Bedu followed a few movements behind, mimicking their motions and forming the words she'd taught him. Chief Llek seemed pleased and addressed the group before him.

"The Monsoon Riders are called to their duty," the chief pronounced. "The river has carried us signs that a village to the north is in danger. They leave today." Chief Llek nodded as if to finalize his statement.

"Chief, with all respect, I have not finished training Nargi and Bargi," Glorya replied, causing a startled response to ripple through the room.

"They have done well enough in the past without your help," Rizku said as he stepped forward, Bunsir translating as quickly as he could. The older man looked worried.

"And they can save even more lives with what I could teach them," Gloria replied, drawing herself up to her full height. The torch light in the hut gleamed like fire on her damp red braids as she spoke. "They are incredibly promising students. Give me one more week with them and they will have mastered the basics of what they need."

The group waited in silence as Rizku studied his opponent. After half a minute of interminable silence, he spoke, his eyes locked onto Glorya's. "Do you know the signs the river gave us?" he asked in a dangerously calm and quiet voice. She shook her head, refusing to look away. "They were bodies. Two women, a child, and a man washed downriver last night. Debris came with them." He paused, gauging Glorya's stunned expression, then continued. "They were not more than a day dead, which tells us they came from the next village upriver. If their flood preparations gave way people could be stranded or worse. We leave within the hour." The large man turned and strode for the door.

"I wish to join you." Glorya's voice surprised even her as her statement froze the room in place. "With the permission of my captain, of course," she added, glancing at Captain Bedu.

He considered warily for a moment, then nodded slowly. "We agreed for you to teach as payment for supplies and housing. If your students must leave, then you must follow." He laid a hand on Glorya's shoulder, earning a small gasp from Bunsir. "Come back to us in one piece," he told her in Zhedaban, and she nodded around a sudden lump in her throat.

"Rizku, what say you?" Chief Llek asked. "Will you have her join your crew for this mission?"

The large man's hawkish eyes narrowed as he studied Glorya, walking a slow circle around her. She stood firm and met his gaze. Finally, Rizku nodded. "She will join Nargi and Bargi's raft," he said as he shoved his way through the tent flap and out into the monsoon. Glorya watched him leave, then deflated as Chief Llek followed. *What have I signed up for?*

You faced a hurricane and won, said a counterpoint voice inside her. *And more people will die if you don't* help. Her resolve stiffened, Glorya nodded to the captain and left to pack what she would need.

An hour later she met Nargi and Bargi at the floating dock on the other side of town. The river before them was swollen to bursting, with the swiftest currents she'd seen on inland water. Logs and branches danced through the swells. "We're navigating that?" she asked Bunsir as she studied the current for an opening—any opening.

The man nodded. "I cannot go with you," he replied, "but you have the beginnings of our language and the respect of some of the team. Trust in their knowledge and instincts—and in your own. The river speaks to us not through our ears, but in our hearts." He made a strange gesture with his hand over his heart and bowed. "You are a Monsoon Rider now. The hope of our people goes with you." Without another word he turned and trudged back toward the village.

Glorya surveyed the rafts tied up to the dock. They had been built out of whatever supplies came to hand, but appeared sturdy nonetheless. Bargi waved to her from the rearmost raft, where he and his brother had just finished securing their gear beneath an awning covering the back half of the raft's deck. Glorya eyed her single oilcloth sack of goods, lifted an eyebrow, and joined them. Bargi grinned as she approached and said something she only half understood over the wind and the language barrier.

"What?" she asked, leaning forward with one ear cupped. The wind around them died down suddenly as Nargi approached. She nodded her approval and thanks as Bargi repeated his statement.

"Glad to see you, Karrilk!" He used the word she'd learned meant "teacher" to greet her, the r's rolling off his tongue like the river over its rocks.

"Good day," she replied, unsure how to voice her trepidation in a way they would understand. She opted for facial expressions instead to convey her skepticism of their ability to navigate the roaring waters. The sturdy raft buckled beneath her as if to underline her unspoken statement.

Bargi laughed and slapped the side of the mast. "Is good! You see." He and Nargi exchanged a few words, then went about the business of making sure preparations were complete to head upstream.

On the other rafts similar preparations were underway. Through the sheets of rain Glorya could just make out slim figures crawling over the decks of two other rafts, untying lines and lashing down supplies. A larger figure loomed suddenly beside the twins' boat, startling Glorya before she recognized Rizku's silhouette against the rainy backdrop. He barked a few words, which Nargi answered in his cooly respectful tone, the one Glorya had come to learn meant he respected the person asking too much to outright call them an idiot despite what he thought. Rizku's responding laugh rang out across the boats, lifting Glorya's spirits a little despite her continued wariness of the man. She bowed politely, but a little less deeply than before, and the shadow returned the gesture in kind before making its way to the lead raft in the procession.

"What did he say?" she asked Nargi after Rizku was out of easy earshot.

"He said you wouldn't come," Nargi replied calmly as he took the tiller in hand and looked to the river ahead. "I told him he was wrong." A small smile lifted the corner of Nargi's mouth as he felt Bargi test the winds, finding a likely one to strengthen to guide them up the river. Bargi joined his brother after helping Glorya stow her own supplies safely beneath a tarp on deck. A whistle cut through the pounding susurration of the rain on the swollen river and all three rafts shoved off.

Glorya felt Nargi and Bargi begin to work the weather as she'd been showing them, first choosing the right winds, then negating the ones in opposition. They struggled for a moment before agreeing on which were most important—and suddenly the rafts surged upstream, dancing nimbly between the trees and debris flung at them. Bargi grinned as they trailed behind the other rafts, watching as they dodged and following in their wake. It was all Glorya could do to figure out where to stand that she wouldn't fall over or get in the way of the tiller. Finally she latched onto a support post near the twins and wrapped an arm around it before casting her own thoughts into the storm that drove them.

She could feel Bargi's influence on the winds that pushed them upstream, without which they would doubtless barely have moved. Nargi was doing a passable job of eliminating crosswinds and headwinds, but Glorya picked apart a few more to help smooth the journey, reaching further forward to make sure the lead raft was covered. Once she'd done all she could for the moment her mind wandered again up into the vast monsoon, stretching across miles and miles of storm without reaching the border. There was a pattern to it; she could see it if she looked far enough. She just needed more time to study it, see what it meant…

"Karrilk!" Bargi was shaking Glorya's shoulder. She blinked owlishly at him, vaguely aware that the raft had stopped. He gestured at the lead vessel, which was stopped a short distance ahead in front of a giant tangle of vegetation and flotsam. Through the continued down-pour she could see the figure of Rizku testing the make-shift dam and realized it blocked a tributary–and that the flotsam was pieces of dwellings and structures with household goods mixed in. There must be a village ahead that's in trouble, Glorya realized, then wondered how they would get through to help.

At a long, shrill whistle, the Monsoon Riders gathered on the middle raft, lashing them together so that they could converse over the wind and rain and not lose any of their vessels to the rough currents. Glorya listened from just outside the loose circle of Temalingari, unable to understand most of the conversation, and chose instead to study the group. Rizku stood a head taller than the largest of his companions, with an incongruously short woman at his side. They bore a striking facial resemblance to each other despite their difference in height, leading Glorya to assume they must be related. Widdershins of the shorter woman was another large man, not as tall as Rizku, but broader, with a serious expression. He appeared to consid-er every word that passed through the group, but spoke lit-tle. To his right was a woman of average height who wore a permanent scowl and appeared slightly older than the rest, with the possible exception of Rizku. Beside her was Bargi, then Nargi, with Glorya standing slightly behind her pupils. She noticed with a start that all of them were barefoot, thinking it an unusual choice for sailing until she realized that their long, flat feet ended in long, thin toes connected by thick webbing. It was all she could do not to stare, so instead she raised her eyes to the conversation at hand.

The discussion within the circle became heated as her attention shifted from the group's appearance to its actions. Rizku seemed to be presenting a plan that garnered an angry outburst from the scowling woman. Bargi spoke up, seeming to support their leader's idea, only to be cut off by the shorter woman beside Rizku. The argument drew out for half a minute before Rizku barked a word to silence the group. He looked to the other large man in the group, who had remained silent during the rest of the conversation, and asked a short question. The man spent a moment in silent consideration, then answered in a few calmly-spoken words that rekindled the scowling woman's outrage. Rizku spoke sharply to her and she cast her eyes downward, still seething, and nodded. Then the group broke apart and headed to their respective rafts.

Nargi nodded to Glorya. "We go back to the village," he said simply as they hopped to their own raft and detached from the flotilla, letting the current shunt them swiftly back the way they'd come. Before long the dock from which they'd left loomed out of the haze of precipitation, and they tied up looking a bit deflated. As they debarked their rafts a small child ran off toward the village, shouting as she went, and by the time they'd retrieved their supplies and made it halfway to town Bunsir met them on the path.

"What happened?" he asked over the wind.

"We ran into a blockage on one of the tributaries," Glorya replied, and he nodded sadly.

"Sometimes that happens," he replied as they turned into the village proper. "The debris is too much for the river to carry, so it lays down its burden where it's found. Sometimes the Monsoon Riders go back with tools and break up the blockage; do you know if that is Rizku's intent?"

Glorya shook her head. "I couldn't make out any of the

planning conversation. You'll have to ask him." Bunsir shifted toward the larger man and asked a few rapid-fire questions, receiving one-word answers for most before drifting back over to Glorya. "He says the blockage is too large for them to remove in time and that the river may yet clear it before the season is over. It's too dangerous even for the Monsoon Riders to attempt." He sighed heavily.

"Are there any other ways to get to the village in need? Other tributaries? Inlets?" Glorya asked, grasping for some way to help.

"We have no vessels to brave the open water, and the storms often make them impassable anyway," Bunsir replied, shaking his head.

Glorya's face lit up. "But we do!" Her companions looked at her askance as she explained. "The Shima carries a longboat for ship-to-shore trips that's outfitted for heavy seas! If there's an inlet that could take us to the village that needs our help, we may could use the longboat to get there! At least," she admitted, "I can ask Captain Bedu. I'm almost certain he'll say yes."

Thirty minutes later the Monsoon Riders joined a small crew from the Shima on the docks. Zem would be responsible for the longboat and her crew and the Monsoon Riders would be responsible for everything else once they'd made land. The longboat would carry provisions for its crew to wait a few days for the Monsoon Riders' return before rejoining the rest of the crew at the Shima in case conditions were difficult on the second inlet. With the help of Bunsir's translations and some primitive maps of the coastline they were able to chart a course a few miles down the coast to the next major inlet in the delta. Rizku felt confident they could reach the struggling village from there.

Captain Bedu's words floated back through Glorya's mind as she helped secure the items in the raft they'd be towing through the choppy seas. It's a fast boat, he'd said, but ill equipped for river travel or debris. Take care the skegs don't get caught on flotsam, too. He'd pondered a moment, then added, A spinnaker would help; I'll speak with Zem about it. A brief silence had fallen between them, thick with intangible, incomplete thoughts, and just as Glorya had started to take her leave, he'd quietly added, Please, take care. I wish to have you back for the return journey. She sensed there was something more to his sentiment than his words implied, but the large man shuttered his expression and turned back to his work.

Now, facing into the roiling wind that would carry them out into the bay, Glorya allowed herself a moment to wonder if she'd be responsible for the death of a dozen people, including herself. But the moment passed quickly as she recalled her trust in the crew, in Zem, and in the judgment of their suddenly enigmatic captain. They would not have all agreed to this if it were suicide. Though they do frequently cross the ocean, which used to amount to same. Mentally shrugging, she caught Bunsir's attention and went to speak with the twins.

Nargi and Bargi were by the tiller of the largest raft of the flotilla. Bargi smiled manically as she approached while his ever-serious brother frowned in consternation, but Glorya ignored both expressions; it was time to be their Karrilk, to let them aid in the mission, sink or swim.

"It's time to put your training to good use," she began through the medium of Bunsir. "I will be with the long-boat, stabilizing the winds from the front; I expect the two of you to handle them for the raft. You worked well together on the river, and I look forward to seeing how you fare out on the bay." She paused and they nodded as one, their expressions matching in grim determination for the first time since she'd met them. They were worried, she guessed, but would never let fear get the best of them when people's lives could hang in the balance.

Satisfied, she gave them a small bow, one which they returned more deeply, and she headed up to the lead vessel to speak with Zem. It was long and sleek, nearly three times as long as it was wide, and today it carried two sails: the usual triangular one amidships and a billowing spinnaker at the fore. Made for speed and stealth, it also carried skegs beneath it to help with stability–which was why they would have to avoid debris from where the river spilled into the bay or risk damaging the skegs and hull. A tow line had been run from the rear of the longboat to a point on the raft behind them. Judging by the choppy seas, it was the only way the raft would be able to fight the out-flow currents to get close to shore, much less upriver.

Zem was performing a few final checks on the tow line as she approached. "Should hold," he said without preamble in his gruff, rough voice. "I must say, Sunchaser, this plan of yours is gutsy, but I think it'll pay off in the end. Plus I have a few tricks up my sleeve that might help." He took Glorya's measure for a moment, then nodded and continued when she met his gaze unflinchingly. "Need you in the longboat. That spinnaker could take us for a ride if something goes wrong."

"I haven't seen one before," Glorya admitted as she felt the small boat buck as if to illustrate the first mate's words. "But I can see the principle behind it. If we lose the raft, I'll kill the wind to it so we can sail properly."

Zem nodded. "If you can do that and leave the main-sail, that'd be best." He gave the rope one last tug, then whistled to the crew, who turned as one toward the boat. Two gestures later the longboat crew was aboard and they were ready to cast off.

Glorya could just make out the Monsoon Riders manning the raft behind them. It was overly crowded, but they'd made makeshift safety lines to keep from falling overboard in the rough seas. She couldn't see their expressions from her vantage, but she could feel Bargi and Nargi testing the winds, pushing and pulling as if they were one mind. Glorya tamped down a swell of pride in her students and turned her own attention to the storm as the lines freed them from the dock's hold. She barely felt the jar of the tow line going taut, trusting to the crew's expertise to carry them through while she focused on her part.

The spinnaker fascinated her as she studied the wind's interactions with it. Whorls of wind slammed into the large cloth, then curled into dense balls of force, ever seeking to get through the barrier of the canvas. Some spilled to either side, bleeding off a small amount of momentum, but the winds caught in the spinnaker's sheet were more than enough to propel the craft at a good speed. The boat angled out just far enough from shore to avoid the crashing waves, then leveled out to look for their target: a large inlet about a mile down the coast.

Abruptly, the wind changed. Where it had been aiding them directly it now hindered, and the spinnaker spun wildly back and forth as if trying to find its way. Glorya felt Bargi reach out and attempt to redirect the flow only to be repulsed sharply by the storm. The monsoon was simply too large and powerful here to redirect. Zem called for the crew to compensate, and they did their best to tack against the wind, but it came at them from all sides, and they found themselves carried further to sea on the tide despite their best efforts. It seemed the weatherworkers would have to find a way.

Sensing Nargi and Bargi watching her, Glorya cast out around the two vessels, finding three main winds in conflict with one another. She tugged at one and felt Nargi pick up the thread, then tugged at another herself and was rewarded with a shift in the spinnaker toward the shore. Keeping hold off the wind she contained, she reached out for the third—and felt Nargi do the same, losing his grip on the first in the process. The spinnaker spun once again as Glorya caught at all three, snuffing them out around both vessels. Free from the crosswinds, the longboat leapt forward once again, the tow line going taut as they progressed more slowly toward land.

They'd made decent progress for a while when another tangle of winds hit them from the side. Longboat and raft listed dangerously for a moment and were carried further out to sea, faster this time than before. Testing the winds, Glorya found the same pattern as last time: three winds directly in conflict, exactly as before. Nargi must have also seen the pattern, for he picked up the same wind he'd negated previously and left the other two for her. Glorya smiled a little as she snuffed out the other two and the craft leveled out once again.

And so it went, down the coast bit by bit, until at last the inlet loomed into view through the rain. Glorya had been parting curtains in the rain along the coast periodically to be sure they didn't miss it. This time Bargi was able to direct more winds into the sails of both craft to help propel them toward the shore. They'd discussed a plan to get the raft down the inlet with some momentum–a brilliant idea from Zem–and now was their moment: they had gained all possible speed, used every trick in the book and all the weatherworking they had, and were pointed directly at the inlet. But at the last moment the longboat turned with surprising agility, bleeding off speed as her dual rudders kicked over hard, and she ran parallel to the coast. The tow line was cut at just the right point, and they watched the Monsoon Riders cheer as their raft was thrown upriver by the momentum, disappearing around a bend faster than they'd have thought possible.

Their task accomplished, the crew pulled in the spinnaker, deciding it was too powerful for good handling with no raft in tow, and beached the longboat just down from the inlet. They'd brought supplies for setting up camp for three nights in case the Monsoon Riders encountered more unexpected difficulties. Glorya was tired as they pitched their small, canvas tents, having fought the weather two more times to get the longboat to shore, but still found the energy to shelter most of the work from the wind before crawling into her own tent and falling fast asleep in the glow of a job well done.

She awoke the following morning to the same gloom, the same constant droning of wind that had dogged them all since the rains came. It usually faded into the background, but this morning as her stomach grumbled at her that she'd skipped dinner, Glorya realized it was more present, more forceful than usual. She pondered this point as she rose, answered the call of nature, and found breakfast: hard tack and some kind of locally-grown fruit. In their hurry to leave they hadn't been picky about their provisions. Chewing thoughtfully (and carefully–the tack was some they'd brought from Zhedaba and was tough even when it was fresh), she returned to her tent and sat in contemplation.

They'd managed to navigate the bay by finding the pattern in the winds and untangling them. Something nagged at the back of Glorya's mind as she turned the pattern over and over again in her head, matching it against everything she'd experienced to date. Nothing fit, and after half an hour of pondering she centered herself determinedly and cast her thoughts far into the monsoon. The answer was there; she knew it.

Immediately she felt the immensity of the system moving over their heads. This time she was able to see not only the local effects but the source of the storms themselves: updrafts that could only mean incredibly tall mountains. The air over the mountains was cold and wild, and it raced toward the coast, razoring through the warmer, tropical air. All manner of effects were born from this headlong dive, and the more she watched, the more Glorya recognized what she was seeing.

By the time Glorya emerged from her tent, she had her answers.

The Shima's crew waited the allotted three days, then shoved off from the beach, looking back periodically at the inlet to make sure no raft sped to meet them. There was an air of apprehension as they sailed back to the dock; few communicated except to sail. Glorya found she had little difficulty this time in keeping the correct winds at bay now that she'd had the time to study the storm. They tied up to the dock earlier than expected and found a small group ready to meet them and help unload.

Glorya found herself looking through the growing throng for…she wasn't sure what, exactly. Or whom. But when Bunsir appeared she headed straight for the man to ask after news of the Monsoon Riders. He chuckled softly and pointed up the trail, where Glorya could just make out the hulking shadow of Rizku through the rain.

"But…how did they get back here?" she asked, thoroughly surprised.

"I don't know all the details," Bunsir explained, "but it seems you all had encountered the blockage from the wrong side. When the blockage is downstream it is much easier to clear. They came back for the other rafts and more supplies now that they know what the trouble is."

"And the villagers?" Glorya prodded when the man went silent. "Are they all right?"

Bunsir deflated a bit as they walked toward town. "Mostly," he replied. "Many have lost livelihoods, and two more have died, but it could have been much, much worse—would have been, had you and your people not done what you did. Chief Llek wishes to speak with you. Your captain is already in town."

To Glorya's surprise, Rizku fell into step beside them on the other side of Bunsir as they made their way into the center of the village. They stopped before the chief's hut, and Rizku turned to face Glorya. She bowed as she always had, expecting the same from him, but was surprised again when he knelt before her. He began to speak, and Bunsir translated automatically, obviously as shocked as Glorya. "Karrilk, you have shown great dedication to your word. You have made it possible for my crew to perform their duties, and have helped save an entire village. Whatever our chief may say, you will always have a place with the Monsoon Riders." Rizku stood, one fist over his heart, and met Glorya's gaze for a moment before turning and entering the chief's hut.

Glorya blinked at Bunsir. The older man blinked back at her, then composed his features and gestured up the steps, also at a loss for words. They entered the chief's chamber together and found Rizku taking up his place behind the man's chair. Captain Bedu was already seated at the table with the chief in awkward, but companionable silence.

Once Gloya and Bunsir were settled, Chief Llek spoke. "I wish to thank you on behalf of all my people," he began. "When we struck this bargain we did not expect to find our visitors nearly as accommodating and helpful as you have been, and the honor of our people demands that we acknowledge an imbalance in our previous arrangement. Your people have helped save a village. Your Karrilk—" he gestured at Glorya—"has taught her students much in a short time, and thanks to the work of your crew we have planted our crops with plenty of time for a good harvest this year. The seas have blessed us richly with your coming." He sat back in his chair and studied the group before him for a moment. "What more would you ask of our people in return? Our original bargain is unequal."

Captain Bedu looked to Glorya for the first time since she'd entered the room, a questioning look in his eye. "What does our Karrilk think?" he asked, the foreign word rolling off his tongue as if it were meant to be there.

Glorya pondered for a moment. "With my captain's permission, I would like leave to return someday and start a weatherworking school," she replied after a moment. "It seems your people could benefit greatly from advanced studies, and I know of a few who might wish to teach here full time." The captain smiled slightly and nodded.

Chief Llek cocked his head to one side. "Yet this is

also something that would benefit my people more than yours," he replied. "It does not even out the scales."

"The school would require you to pay for the teachers and provide them with homes, and would also take students out of the fields and off the rivers to study," Glorya pointed out. "A worthwhile investment, but one that does not come cheap in the short term."

Chief Llek pondered for a moment, then nodded. "You are correct. It does balance the scales…to a point. But what can we do for you?" he asked, indicating the captain and Glorya.

Captain Bedu cleared his throat quietly. "I understand you have a contraption here that can help predict the rains," he said demurely. "A glass filled with water and some other substance that tells your people when it will rain and when it will be dry."

The chief nodded. "It is a contraption of my son's design. Do you wish one for yourself?" At the captain's nod, Chief Llek gestured to Bunsir. "Please make certain the captain receives a weather glass. The best you can find."

"Thank you," Captain Bedu said, smiling genuinely. "I have found them very intriguing, and one does not always have a weatherworker nearby to warn of rough seas." His gaze slid to Glorya, and for a moment his smile flashed bittersweet before he turned his attention once again to their host.

"If that is all you require, beyond the original arrangement of supplies and boarding during the storms, then we have a deal," the chief said. "I believe your people shake hands on these things…"

Captain Bedu stood, extending his hand across the table for Chief Llek to grasp awkwardly for a moment, then let go. "Indeed, Chief. We have a deal."

For six more weeks the Shima rode out the monsoons. The crew aided the villagers in everyday tasks, many learning the basics of the language, and a few even began to learn the intricate glassworking that pervaded every structure in the village. By the time the weather cleared enough for them to set sail nearly every crew member—and many of the villagers—had forged friendships and learned enough from one another to make the day of their departure more difficult than they'd anticipated. One or two of the crew members even decided to stay behind, having found a home in this foreign place. But the rest began the arduous task of readying the ship for the two month voyage home.

Glorya found herself too busy to think about leaving behind her pupils. She and the Monsoon Riders had spent as much time as possible in port this season, and it seemed whatever river deity they worshipped was merciful enough to let them. She'd managed to make accomplished weatherworkers of both of them and was certain they saw her as something of a wise older sister at this point. She had to admit she'd grown fond of their antics and was more proud of them than she could put into words. But it was time for them to continue on their own, and she had planted the seed of an idea that would help make sure their people could manage whatever the weather threw at them.

For that matter, she had a few ideas that would make the world an easier and better place for people like herself: weatherworkers who needed and wished to make a living. But she had to get home before she could make any of them a reality.

Finally, all the preparations were finished, and the crew

found themselves on the dock at the edge of town in the misting rain, bidding farewell to friends and acquaintances. The entire town had turned out to see the Shima off. Well-wishers filled the beach in a thick semicircle that covered a quarter mile in each direction with Chief Llek and Bunsir at the apex. Captain Bedu strode down the gangplank and onto the beach to personally thank the chief for his hospitality and was surprised when the man gripped his forearm in a gesture of thanks and familiarity. He recovered quickly and returned the gesture with a genuine smile. Bunsir blinked rapidly as Glorya approached to say her goodbyes.

"You have been such a help to me," she began in Temalingari—and found herself sniffling as Bunsir barely held back tears. "Thank you."

"It is I who must thank you," he replied. "You have helped us in more ways than you know." Glorya could tell he wanted to say more, but had neither the words nor the ability to say more. She nodded and smiled, blinking back tears of her own, then turned to Bargi and Nargi, who were waiting nearby.

"Karrilk," they said as one, kneeling in the sand. Glorya snorted at the tops of their heads.

"Please, rise," she said, almost reaching out to help them up from the sand, then remembering herself. "You have learned all I can teach you, and I am proud to have been your Karrilk." They rose as one, beaming their pride in her praise. Bargi grinned at his brother, who turned back to Glorya.

"We cannot convince you to stay, can we?" he asked. "I still feel we have much to learn."

Glorya smiled softly at her former charges. "There are some things I must do," she replied, "but I will give you this one last lesson: never stop learning. Never stop questioning, and always ask 'why' until you get an answer you can use." She bowed respectfully to both, then looked up and down the line of villagers. Rikzu and the rest of the Monsoon Riders nodded to her, and she nodded in return. And then there were no more goodbyes left to give.

Captain Bedu joined her as she strode back toward the Shima and home.

Early summer saw them returned to the coastal waters of Zhedaba. The trip back had gone as well as the trip to Temalingar, and they'd made good time despite being laden with provisions and trade goods—the villagers had done their best to see to it there wasn't a single unused space in the hold. Consequently, the captain was concerned when a sail appeared on the horizon just outside the protection of the shipping lanes.

Calling Glorya to his side, he pointed out the approaching ship, a grim expression on his face. "I knew they'd be back," he growled. "That's the same ship we outran on the trip out. The difference is, this time we're too full to outrun her." He studied Glorya for a moment. "Any ideas?"

She thought for a moment. "Do you know her captain?" she asked quietly. The question took the captain aback, but he responded easily enough.

"Not personally, but by reputation and experience. He's known as The Butcher; he never leaves his opponents alive, and is often known to do worse before he kills them." His eyes narrowed. "Why do you ask?"

Glorya nodded. "Give me a moment," she said as she moved to the fantail, closing her eyes. She could feel the captain a curious, but respectful distance away, close enough to help if something went wrong. And then her thoughts were in the winds behind the ship, flowing down the strands of force that powered the sails above her. Those same strands led her awareness to the furls she associated with sails. She'd had an idea she'd wanted to test for some time at scale, but hadn't had the chance; it seemed this was her moment.

She opened her eyes and instantly found the sails on the horizon behind them. Casting her will out across the gap, she created a bubble of no-weather the size of the ship, much as she'd done in the desert sandstorms to save the people she traveled with, only this time she anchored it.

To the deck of the ship.

Almost instantly the sails began to slip from view as the Shima easily outran her pursuers. Glorya heard Captain Bedu suck in a breath as the trailing ship slipped over the horizon, and he narrowed his eyes further.

"What exactly did you do?" he asked warily.

"I stopped the wind," she replied, looking him full in the face. "No wind will ever move that ship again." Turning on her heel, Glorya left the quarterdeck, the captain's gaze burning a hole in her back until she was out of sight belowdecks.

The next day they pulled into the docks in Jogete. Captain Bedu had not spoken to Glorya since she'd stopped their pursuers, and it made her nervous; he was nothing if not a principled man, and she still wrestled with her own conscience over her actions. Doldrums could be fatal for a crew. Now that they had arrived at their destination she felt she had to find a way to speak to the man, to make things right. She respected him too much to do otherwise.

Glorya found the captain in his quarters, signing manifests for their cargo. He looked up momentarily as she entered. "Sunchaser," he grunted from behind his pile of paperwork. "To what do I owe the pleasure?"

Glorya gestured her apology and spoke in Zhedaban. "I wish there to be no misunderstanding between us on account of my actions yesterday," she began, and the captain shook his head, gesturing for her to stop. She trailed off, waiting for an explanation that was a few long moments coming.

"You did what was right for this crew," Captain Bedu replied, "and you acted based on my estimation of our enemy. If there is fault or guilt, it is mine." He made a warding gesture she didn't quite recognize, then continued. "I have already sent word to the port authority that there is a becalmed ship beyond the shipping lanes in need of help." At this Glorya's eyebrows rose and she felt a weight lift from her heart. "Please do not trouble yourself about it any longer."

"Thank you, sir," Glorya replied. "I was concerned you were angry with me." A strange silence stretched between them as the captain seemed lost for words for a moment.

"I was...surprised," he explained lamely. "It seemed out of character for you, and I was concerned you might have caused yourself guilt you would feel the rest of your life." At this his expression became haggard, and she suspected he spoke more of his own experiences than hers. Drawing a hand over his face, he continued. "Please think no more of it. I am grateful you were able to make such a choice in service to my crew.

"Speaking of crew, I have your pay." He extended a hefty sack across his desk. It was larger than she expected and seemed to contain more than simple coin.

"It is too much," she said, taking it and weighing the

contents in her palm. "Definitely more than we agreed upon when I was hired."

"That was before we made the most profitable run we've seen yet thanks to you." Captain Bedu stood and moved around from behind his desk. His clothing was rumpled, as if he'd slept in it the night before and not gotten around to changing; it was an out of character look for him. He extended a hand, and Glorya shook it firmly. As he let go a strange look crossed his face, and a wry smile twisted his lips. "If I were a younger man…" He shook his head, running a hand through his hair. "But alas, I am not, and for all I could wish otherwise you're not the type to stay in one place long." He sighed as Glorya processed what she was hearing. "Still, if you ever find yourself in need of anything and I am able to render assistance, come find me. I'm sure you'll know how." And with that he sat back down at the desk and turned back to his paperwork.

"Goodbye, sir," Glorya replied softly as she stowed her pay with the rest of her worldly belongings in her satchel. "And thank you." With that, she turned and, with more difficulty than she'd thought possible, made her way out of the cabin and down the gangplank of the ship.

It was time to go home.

ALSO BY
EMILY BARLOW

STORMKINDLER
(BOOK TWO OF
THE WEATHERWORKER CHRONICLES)

THE RAVEN'S CHILDREN

INVOLUNTARILY IMMORTAL

Stormkindler

In the shadowy winds off the north coast of Midlands, a sinister plot brews on a ship poised to pounce, threatening the fates of thousands unaware of the danger lurking just beyond their shores.

Enter Glorya Sunchaser, a formidable name across the lands, as she returns to school after years in the field. She accompanies her niece Zayira, a gifted but unconventional student, whom she promises to protect as she attends the only weatherworking school in the realm: Weatherwatch. But as Zayira struggles to find her place, Glorya steps into the daunting shoes of her late mentor, who left behind not only a legacy but a dangerous mystery that could change everything. With time running out, Glorya must unravel his secrets before they fall into malevolent hands. Can they navigate the perilous tides of magic and betrayal, or will darkness consume them both?

Dive into this thrilling tale where loyalty, courage, and destiny collide!

The Raven's Children

In a kingdom teetering on the edge of chaos, three siblings — Ambjorg, Asbjorn, and Audolf — watch helplessly as their father, King Hrafn, succumbs to illness. With shadows lurking and treachery afoot, the throne is under threat from sinister forces eager to seize power.

As strange and monstrous beasts begin to attack their realm, the siblings find themselves entangled in a web of duty, secrets, and their extraordinary bond with animals. Forced to step into unfamiliar roles, they must navigate fierce rivalries and uncover dark truths to protect their loved ones and save their kingdom.

Join Ambjorg, Asbjorn, and Audolf in a gripping tale of courage, loyalty, and the fight against an unseen enemy. Will their unique gifts be enough to restore peace, or will they lose everything they hold dear?

Discover the heart-pounding adventure where family ties are tested and destinies are forged!

Involuntarily Immortal

Sable Montgrief wishes her curse would let her die. Unfortunately for her, fate has other plans.

Sable longs for release from her centuries-old fate. Living alone in a remote cabin, she's close to breaking the spell keeping her alive—until her solitude is shattered by a desperate father, Adem Ozturk.

Adem is in a race against time to save his daughter, Ailith, who is haunted by terrifying visions of a future she cannot control. Their only hope lies with Sable, whose unique abilities could prevent a coming catastrophe—but convincing her to help means binding her to another lifetime of torment.

Dive into a gripping tale of sacrifice, fate, and the thin line between life and death in this spellbinding urban fantasy adventure!

About the Author

A software architect by day, Emily enjoys reading, writing, knitting, crocheting, sewing, running, and learning martial arts with her family in her spare time. She is supported by her longtime husband and two wonderful children, who endure her eccentricities with enthusiasm.

For more information and to join her mailing list, visit https://emilybarlowwritesthings.com or scan the QR code below!

www.ingramcontent.com/pod-product-compliance
Lightning Source LLC
Chambersburg PA
CBHW050454110726
47899CB00003B/939